PLAYING

HOUSE

A Black Widow Novel

Playing House
By Christa Simpson

Copyright © 2015 Christa Simpson

Electronic Edition
ISBN: 978-1-926478-08-1

Paperback Edition
ISBN: 978-1-926478-11-1

ALL RIGHTS RESERVED.

Cover Design by Christa Simpson
Editor: Lia Fairchild

Black Widow Publishing: August 2017

CHRISTA SIMPSON

BWP BlackWidow Publishing

No men were harmed in the making of this novel.

Dark Secrets, A Duet

Part One

Join Christa's Author Newsletter to receive special news, sneak previews, limited-time freebies, and exclusive offers right in your inbox.

See what you're missing out on!
http://christasimpson.com/newsletter

1: Life As I Know It

I gnorance truly is bliss. My car pulls away from the curb, my tousled hair dancing in the wind as if our autumn is unseasonably warm. You can't believe everything you see. In all honesty, it's not that warm. I have a chill running through my body that I can't escape. I probably would have closed up my car window a long time ago, if I could have, but it's stuck halfway down. I'm just lucky the raincloud over there is keeping its distance. *Lucky.* Hah! I'm *lucky* like that man up ahead.

Look at his tidy pile of leaves. He probably spent his entire morning raking those things into a heap next to the curb and is proud of himself for beating the rain. I smirk at the rotund, older man in his front yard. He hasn't even had enough time to put away his rake. Instead, he stands there proudly, leaning against the handle and scratching his overfed belly. I can't resist. Someone has handed this opportunity to me, and I simply can't pass it up.

My foot presses deeper into the accelerator, thrusting my small car forward. I glare at the old man from beneath dark lashes. His eyes immediately connect with mine, begging me to rethink what I'm about to do. That only encourages me further. I veer toward the pile, blasting through the leaves and cheering with a crazed depth to my voice.

"Woooooo!"

I feel so alive. When the old man stumbles after me, frantically waving his hands with leaves raining around him, I smile harder. *A smile.* For the longest time, I forgot my mouth could even do that. It feels like my world has shifted, though, and maybe, just maybe things are looking up for me. I force the images of my tormented childhood down, forgetting about my mother's wasted apologies and the gurgling sound that came from my father's throat when he drowned before my very eyes. I've blown through enough of my life boo-hooing over them. No more.

I carry on down the road, wearing a real smile—not the fake one I wore throughout my unfortunate youth, being spread between perverted foster fathers and overbearing relatives who wanted to make themselves feel better by sporadically treating me like family. No, remembering how I was pawned off to the system never helps. This is why my smiles never last long.

With a deep breath, my smile wilts, but I remind myself that I'm not a teenager anymore. I'm finally free of those people and their unanswered promises. No one's in charge of my destiny but me. I have to grab life by the balls and make shit happen. Just because my late parents had a few screws loose, doesn't mean I have to be stuck in my own self-inflicted hell, right? *Right?*

I pause at a yellow light and proceed into the intersection, flicking on my left turn signal as I make the turn in front of an oncoming sports car. It's a dumb move. Traffic is thick, and the dude driving the small, black car is in a hurry to go nowhere. He swerves around my rear bumper and lays on his horn. I flip him the bird and hold it there for a few long seconds, completely lost in my own world. I forget to reacquaint myself with the car in front of me. Traffic is now at a standstill.

I quickly jam onto my brake, but I'm screwed. My balding tires argue with the pavement and make a loud screeching noise while my front-end slams into the car in front of me. A loud popping noise is the only warning I have before wearing a face full of airbag. I don't care if it looks like a fluffy cloud; it feels like a brick wall, and I wonder if I have a broken nose. I struggle to breathe as I push the bag out of my face and clutch at my nose, sighing deeply, choking on the stale air.

Way to go, Clarisse.

"Are you okay?" a man shouts, reaching through my half-open window and tearing my car door from its hinges to pull me free of the wreckage. He thinks my window is broken because of the accident, and I'm going to let him keep on thinking that.

I'm still holding my nose when I collapse into his arms and look up into apologetic eyes. "I've had better days," I admit.

"But you're alive."

The corners of my lips quirk upwards oh so slightly. "There's that."

He helps me right myself, and I push off of him once I regain my footing. "My bumper didn't even see you coming," he says with a smile.

I assess the damage. My shitty little car is banged up pretty good, but it'll drive. The back end of his car sits on the ground in a heap of ruin. "Is it true that they can pick that thing up and reattach it?" I ask, already knowing the answer.

"I don't know. See the way the fender is curled under. That'll be a hard fix."

I nod, wondering if I should throw my entire first year of college away and run for the hills. The dark cloud that had been following me finally catches up. My eyes wander to the bystanders who scatter for cover as droplets of rain start to pelt the pavement.

"I can't afford to fix your car." I look back to him, trying not to admire his clean-cut military hairstyle. "I'm sorry but I just can't."

His eyes sink into mine while he thinks on it, the rain quickly dampening his clothes and mine. He takes my hand to get my attention. It works.

"What do you say we talk to these nice policemen over here and then I take you out for a coffee? I'm sure we can work something out.'

2: Ignorance is Bliss

"**M**ove in with me, Clarisse." Finlay moves in close and whispers intimately against my ear.

I laugh and push him away because I'm stunned. We haven't been dating all that long. I quickly hide my reaction when I notice how serious he's being. If the rickety wooden swing we were sitting on hadn't been rocking gently, I wouldn't have been able to hide my jittery hands. "You're serious?"

"Dead serious."

"But we've only been dating for a few months now." I don't think his insurance company has even paid him for his extensive car repairs yet, but his soft brown eyes beg me to say yes anyways.

"I love you, Clarisse." His serious expression doesn't change and neither does the firm line of his jaw. He plants both of his feet on the ground, and it stops all motion, but my head keeps swinging as he speaks. "When school's back in, we won't be able to see each other as much. Is that what you want?"

I shake my head, still too stunned by the sudden proposal to form a complete sentence. "But... but..."

A smirk replaces that serious look on his face. "I've already contacted the Admissions Department and all of our classes for next semester are a match."

I nibble on my lower lip and gloss over that fact for a few seconds. A little odd—maybe even too good to be true—as many things tend to be right before they turn to shit. I should know. My life is about to land in a really big pile of the stinky stuff, and there isn't a damn thing I can do about it.

"Come on," he says, tearing me from my thoughts.

I nod and get in the car—the same car I had practically demolished mere months ago. I ignore the seatbelt at first, but when Finlay starts weaving through traffic at a high speed, I secretly secure it over my shoulder. Within another five minutes of his maniacal city driving, he parks his car on a tight street with tall pastel houses and short driveways. He gets out of the car, pulls open my door, and helps me to the sidewalk. I grip on to his gloved hand and look up into his eyes, curiosity getting the better of me.

"Where are we?" My stomach roils, like a hollow ball of pain, because I know Finlay is up to something here, and I don't know what it is.

Finlay stops me dead in my tracks and holds up a finger, not ready to let the cat out of the bag just yet. "Give me one second." He jogs through someone's front yard and plucks a small winter flower from the lawn. He walks back toward me grinning like a fool, and I meet him halfway.

He shows me the small flower. "I love you," he says, offering it to me.

I look at the small, purple flower dwarfed between his index finger and thumb. Most people would call it a weed, but when he waits expectantly for me to take it, the little, purple flower might as well be a dozen long-stemmed roses. I take it and smile. For one stolen moment, he makes me forget about first impressions and meeting the parents.

His lips come down on mine gently. They're forgiving and tender at first, but what starts out as something affectionate and sweet, turns into a deeply intimate kiss that has me drinking from his mouth and angling my head to swallow him whole. This is when his mother opens her front door.

I glance up with puckered lips and half-lidded eyes, cowering into my scarf with a yelp and a swear word cut off by my shock of finding her standing there with her arms folded across her chest. Her face remains very stern. So that's where he gets his prominent jawline from.

Finlay takes my hand and pulls me toward the glowering woman. "Clarisse, I'd like you to meet my mother."

I stumble over my own two feet until I find solid ground beneath them. "Finlay, do you think I could see you over here for just a minute? Excuse us," I say to his mother, dragging him back down the sidewalk.

There will be no forgiveness from her. I check back over my shoulder to make sure I'm not hallucinating, but the tightness of her jaw proves I am not.

I try to whisper, but I start rambling anxiously. "What can I say? I was not expecting this."

"And... what's the problem, exactly?" Finlay asks me.

I scratch the back of my head and cringe, passing it off as a chill. "You're the first steady thing I've ever known in a life full of ups and downs—mostly downs." I glance down at my boots, but he lifts my chin.

"Come on, Clarisse. My mom's invited you to dinner. This is important. We're going to tell her tonight. You can't say no." Finlay's full-pouting smile is all he needs to reel me in and make for damn sure that I can't say no.

I'm extremely nervous. "Tell her what, exactly?"

"School comes back in soon and I've decided to move back home," he says. "I'm planning on telling her that tonight. She'll be ecstatic."

I just barely stop my jaw from hitting the ground. "About you, maybe."

He shakes his head and grips on to my chin a little too strongly. "My mom is going to love you. I want you to move in with us, too. Is that not what you want?"

He asks so many damn questions. I don't see what the rush is. Why does he always have to put me on the spot like this? I flip over another idea in my head. I could go back to my hole in the ground—alone—but where will that get me?

I answer him with a nod because I'm not opposed to living with him, and this house looks a lot nicer than the dump I'm currently staying at, but I'm afraid his mother won't be as easily persuaded.

Finlay reassures me in every way he can. His hand squeezes mine. "We aren't going to see each other as much as we have been. I don't like that very much. Are you not okay with this? I thought it was going to be a nice surprise."

When I hesitate, he keeps talking, as if my avoidance of the question isn't a slap across the face.

"You'll be closer to school and we can spend more time

together."

Without thinking of another lame excuse, I take my first real chance at a new life. "I'm ready and, as long as your mother is onboard, I'm okay with this."

"You are?" He's surprised I agreed, and frankly so am I.

"Yeah," I repeat, certain that this is the best move for me.

He reaches for my hand, looking like he's ready to take me back to his mother, but then he leans over and claims my mouth, clutching my head, not wanting to let me go. At first, he slows his lips, and then he deepens the kiss again before breaking free for a breath and a smile. I smile back.

There's the reason why I'm saying yes.

He whispers next to my ear. "I love you, Clarisse."

Those words tie my stomach in knots, and those knots don't loosen for the rest of evening. It's not until I've struggled through the awkward dinner conversation and received the third degree from his mother over dishes that I get to settle on my heels and take a much needed breath.

Finlay can see I need a break from his mother. "Come on. Let's go downstairs." He takes my hand and hauls me toward the basement door, smiling back at me. The second my socked feet reach the cold basement floor, he tugs me into a hug. For two whole seconds, I feel completely secure—happy even.

"Come." Finlay pulls me across the room to the entertainment area where he drops to his knees in front of me. "Thank you for everything tonight. My mom really likes you. I think this is going to be great."

I smirk, running my hand over the short hairs on his head. "You really think so? I don't know."

"She does," he insists while he digs through a drawer of adapters and remote controls.

"I'm sure she treats all of your girlfriends like this."

Finlay snaps to his feet and twists to face me. "You're the only one, Clarisse. I've never brought a girl back to meet my family before. I don't want to hear you ever say anything like that again."

I wasn't expecting such an intense response. He's

breathing heavier. Darkness seeps into his eyes. I'm starting to believe that maybe his family life isn't as picture perfect as his mother lets on. I'm stunned into a silence that makes me shiver. Finlay's expression lightens when he catches the surprise in my eyes. He scoops a blanket from the back of the sofa and tosses it on the basement floor, and when he looks back to me, the darkness has already begun to fade.

"You're special to me, Clarisse. That's all. You're not like the other college girls."

He's got that much right. I'm nothing like the other girls. I'm *different*. You'll never catch me staring at every passing mirror, worrying about my hair or the color of my lip gloss. I live in reality. I worry about where my next meal is coming from and where I'll lay my head. I do my best to hide my weaknesses and pride myself on how far I've come on my own, but right now, I just want to be the girl he thinks I am.

"Are you going to spend the night with me?" His question knocks me off kilter, but I know what I'm agreeing to if I say yes.

I swallow back my nerve and kneel next to him on the blanket, my heart thundering in the silence. I look up into his eyes submissively, the silence swirling around us like a whirlpool.

"Yeah?" he asks, the softness of his voice touching me.

I nod.

Wearing his resulting smile, Finlay flicks on his Smart TV and scrolls for a movie—any movie. He turns it up a little on the loud side and kneels close to me. There's a charge in the room when our eyes connect, and I know we're both thinking about getting intimate. Heat creeps down my neck. My heart hammers against my ribcage. *This is finally happening.*

His smile does things to me as he moves in closer yet, first grabbing my hand and then drawing his mouth to mine for a kiss that steals my breath. My eyes flutter shut, and I battle for sanity as he hooks on to my bottom lip and tugs at it with his teeth. He wraps his arms around my waist for a squeeze before sliding his hands under my shirt to unhook my bra and massage me intimately.

Pinning me against him, Finlay takes all of my weight into his arms and twirls me around, flattening me on the floor beneath him. I rake my fingers through his short hair, his mouth possessing mine. This isn't like our other kisses, either. *This is me saying yes.*

His body presses into mine in places that ache to be touched by him. Once he covers himself with another blanket he'd dropped on the floor next to us, his hands skim back to my waist and play with the band of my yoga pants. He smiles and lets out a content sigh.

"Are you sure you're ready for this?" His voice is a little husky. He's just as nervous as I am.

I nod and he instantly pecks at my mouth, hovering over me like he's experienced at the task. I know he's not, from what I hear, and it just makes this moment that much more special.

He keeps kissing me, his hands roaming over my body to pull my pants over each hip. I don't know when he got his own pants off, but I can suddenly feel skin against skin. The foreign warmth drives me mad in the best kind of way.

"You're so soft," he whispers, trailing kisses from my ear to my neck to my throat. His fingers whisper over my hip and slide down to the juncture between my thighs. Air whooshes out of his mouth when I spread my legs for him and let him cup a very sensitive place.

I lift my hips up to meet him and grind against his palm, begging for more pressure. He gives it to me for a moment but quickly pulls away. I cry out from the loss, gasping for a breath and holding it there, hoping his mother hasn't heard me from upstairs. Finlay smiles when he replaces his hand with a very erect appendage. He slides against me—the solid length of him making promises I hope he can keep.

A full body tremor takes me into a state of expectation. I want this so badly now that I'm aching from the inside out. My thighs tremble with anticipation and nerves.

"I've been waiting a long time for this," he says. His hand disappears under my shirt, discovering curves on my body he's now allowed to touch freely.

I suck in a breath when he pinches my taut nipple. The stinging sensation only heightens my arousal. "What if it hurts?" I whisper on an exhale.

He kisses me on the lips and then rolls on the condom he retrieves from his jeans' pocket. He strokes his long shaft a few times, looking down at me. "It's not going to hurt." He licks at his bottom lip and positions himself at my throbbing entrance. "I love you."

He comes down and connects our mouths in a heated kiss, pressing forward in one fluid motion, uniting us body and soul. His hips back out slowly, testing my limits before plunging forward again. I whimper when he does it. It fucking hurts. He's just as long as he looks, and hard like steel. The next time it hurts again, but dare I say it hurts good? After a few more long strokes, I wrap my legs around his waist and squeeze, holding my breath, tightening around him, and wanting more of that deep penetration— needing it. I pant in sync with his every stroke.

"Oh God," I whisper against his lips, out of pleasure.

"Is this good?" he asks, just as his mother comes jogging down the stairs.

My eyes bulge open, and I drop my legs to the floor, waiting for Finlay to roll aside, but he's unmoveable, stiffened inside me, his arms in a push-up.

His mother stops at the bottom of the stairs. "Oh, sorry guys," she says, waving a hand as if to block her view.

"Mom," Finlay grumbles, flexing his ass muscles and sinking in deeper.

I want to shout out how good it feels, but she's watching me. Even though we're covered with a blanket, I think it's pretty obvious what we're doing. I have to believe the intrusion is intentional, but she grabs whatever it is she acts like she needs from the closet and scurries back upstairs humming a tune like she hasn't just found her son poking me on her basement floor.

Finlay doesn't seem to skip a beat. He starts to move again, connecting our mouths at the same time, and even though it seems a little awkward at first, the more he moves the better it begins to feel. He continues with a slow and steady pump of his hips and a showering of sensual kisses that take me to the next level. When he presses a little deeper, I lift off the floor gasping for air, loving the tight sensation I create.

"I'm sorry. Are you okay?" he blurts. Finlay looks so worried that he's hurt me, frozen in place, his body held taught above me.

I erupt into a nervous giggle and smile widely. "I'm okay," I say, feeling much better than okay. "How are you?"

He presses deeply into me. "This place—right here—is my new favorite place to be."

Finlay starts to plunge forward with a renewed force. I find myself spreading my legs wider, with my hands on my inner thighs so I can feel him slap against me with every thrust. I wrap my legs around him, and we both groan softly from the new tightness we've discovered. He checks me over, smirking as his body continues to crush into mine.

I only whimper, feeling my body mounting for something new and amazing.

"Talk to me, baby. Does this feel good?" He sounds short of breath when he presses dangerously hard against my clitoris.

"Yes!" I shout as his hand comes down over my mouth, surrounded by the remnants of my shattered virginity.

He smiles with an open mouth, making me spiral with arousal as he rapidly moves his hips. His body tightens as I come undone beneath him, clenching and releasing, gasping for air and clinging onto him as if my life depends on it. Then he flattens me to the floor and digs deep, whispering my name as he stiffens and then falls over me.

"Clarisse."

A cloud of contentment swaddles me and, for a few minutes, I'm truly convinced I've made the right decision and waited for the right person. While I right my clothes, Finlay presses a kiss into my lips, marking the end of my independence. Clarisse Blackwell is no longer a virgin. I like how it feels, but I don't like the look in Finlay's eyes—the look that says he's now owner of my freedom. Things are good, though, so I let him believe that I'm his while an inkling of regret wiggles its way into my heart.

I keep that bundled away with all my other mental baggage for the ensuing weeks. I cram my belongings into a small closet in Finlay's bedroom and settle in for the holidays. Finlay goes back to being a dream come true. He's kind and sweet and thoughtful. We spend time together, curled up in front of fireplaces, exploring the big city and making love like animals. Everything seems so new and exciting, but then school resumes. That's when everything changes.

It's amazing what people can disguise so cleverly in public when they really, really want to—even in private for a short while. Now that Finlay has me, it's a new game we're playing. He's the player, I'm the pawn, and no one gets to run interference in this game.

3: My Mistake

The sky is filled with clouds this morning, but a ray of winter sunshine peeks out from behind them. I tilt my head in an attempt to absorb that small bit of sunshine, just as it's snuffed by the clouds. Finlay pulls into the college parking lot, finds a spot to park, and leaps out of the car. When I open my door, I sink behind my scarf to hide from the whipping wind. I move around the front of the car quickly but still have to run across the road to catch up to Finlay. He's in a hurry to get nowhere, apparently. He heads in the opposite direction of our classroom.

He clasps onto my hand when I reach him. "I have to stop by admissions. Something's wrong with my schedule and I couldn't fix it online."

"Okay." Not a big deal, except that he hadn't told me about it sooner.

I shrug it off and keep the smile pasted on my face. We're not far from the Admissions Department anyway, so we head straight there. We enter the building, walk down the hall, and wait our turn in the lineup. It shouldn't take too long, from the look of the small crowd of students in the waiting area, but I could stare into his eyes all day and say nothing at all, so we're set.

He leans down and kisses me. "Love you."

"Four seventy-two!" the lady shouts when Finlay misses his number.

Finlay snaps out of it instantly, gets up, and turns back to tell me, "You can wait here. I'll only be a minute." He retrieves his hand from mine and walks up to the available clerk.

I smile at the person sitting in the waiting area next to us and step aside, feeling childish and putdown by the way he treated me. Still, I keep my head held high. I respect his privacy and let him approach the desk alone.

The middle-aged woman wearing a tight bun at the base

of her neck looks up at Finlay expectantly. "Can I help you?"

Finlay slaps down an unfolded piece of paper and smooths it out in front of her, poking a pointed finger into the page. "What is this?"

She reads for a moment, quickly locates his student ID, types sporadically into her keyboard, and peers over her reading glasses at the screen. She lifts her tablet off the stand and, after a few swipes of her finger, turns it around to show Finlay. "This one class can't be switched. There is no availability. See here?"

Finlay reaches for the device, but the woman pulls it away, replaces it on her desk, and settles back in her chair, as if that might end the conversation. I keep my distance, knowing it's far from over.

Finlay shakes his head. "What do you mean you switched my schedule? You can't just mess with a student's schedule. I did not authorize this." He starts pulling at his hair and squeezing his eyes shut, his face contorting into a frustrated twist. This is a new side of Finlay, and I don't like it very much.

The woman scowls back at him from behind her large desk. "There's a note right here that your request to be in all of Ms. Blackwell's classes would be approved only if the class size allows for it. The requests were all approved except for Physiology of Fitness. I'm sorry, Mr. Turnbull, but that's the best we can do for you."

Finlay turns his back to me, blocking the screen and leaning forward so he can see for himself, keeping his voice low. "I don't know what you're talking about. I understood we were in all the same classes." His eyes drill into hers to make a point. I'm not to hear this conversation.

Oh, but I already have.

The woman keeps her eyebrows raised high and her tone clipped. "Turns out you were wrong, Mr. Turnbull." She glances at Finlay over her small glasses with a disapproving look on her face. She's not prepared to back down. She obviously doesn't know Finlay very well, and I'm starting to believe that neither do I.

"I'm sure you can fix this," he insists, turning on the charm and leaving his cold threats in the dust. He reaches over the desk and adjusts the woman's name tag. "A woman in your position must have her ways, Greta."

Right when I think she's going to sock him one, she comes up with a question more shocking. "What is it you want to be when you're done with school, Mr. Turnbull?"

"A chiropractor," he states. "But I don't see what that has to do with anything."

She smiles with pasty pink lips, but it looks like it's painful for her to do so. "I'd love to teach you something no physiology class ever will—it's called respect—but I'm afraid I don't have the time and you don't have the patience to make any progress on that front today."

I don't like the way this conversation is turning, with Finlay growing more suspicious, glancing over his shoulder to see whether I've heard any of that or not. There's a tightness in his jaw that would actually be quite attractive if he weren't growing angrier by the second. To stop the impending doom, I act like I've missed their entire conversation, smile and turn away. Inside, though, I flounder with the idea that he is the reason our schedules are nearly a complete match.

The school day resumes, and I keep a lock down on my curiosity. Even though Finlay fights again with the admissions department to fix the unmatched class issue the next day, and the next, it doesn't work. I act unaffected by his lies and, for the remainder of our first week back, I focus on remaining calm while I'm a total mess inside. Another week of classes comes and goes.

"Come on. Class is about to start." I tug Finlay to our last class of the day, and don't stop until we're inside one of the classroom doors flanking the front of the room.

Many other students file into the room around us. I've no doubt we've all heard the same rumor about our professor. When class starts, he'll lock the doors. No one will be allowed in the room after that, under any circumstances.

We hustle up the stairs in the lecture hall, hand in hand.

Half way into the room, I slide between the long desks and take a seat toward the middle. Two of Finlay's buddies come walking in the same entrance that we had. Luke, the dark haired one, gives me a small wave before taking the seat beside Finlay. I smile and wave, and Finlay doesn't seem to have a problem with that, but when the vacant seat to my left gets eyed up by a very handsome, very blond, classmate, things get ugly.

"Hey," I say, smiling at the guy when he walks toward me. It'd be rude not to. It's not because he's attractive, with hair as white as ice, although I'm not the only woman looking his way when he speaks to me with a clean European accent.

"I remember you," he says, smiling.

"Oh?" I say, returning the smile.

"Ryan," he says, reaching his hand out to me. "I don't believe we've been formally introduced."

"Shhh!" The sound whooshes from Finlay's mouth as a warning.

In that moment, I know I had better not take his hand. The introduction ends there, the greeting remaining one-sided, unfinished and awkward.

It's fine. The beautiful man doesn't need to tell me where he remembers me from. How could I have missed him two desks over in our physiology class the other day? It was the one class I didn't have Finlay breathing down my neck the entire time. Despite Finlay's obvious disapproval of our connection, Ryan takes the seat next to me, and I'm not talking two seats down. No, literally right beside me, close enough that our arms bump when we start taking notes moments later.

"Oh, sorry," I say, feeling like a doofus. Being left-handed has its disadvantages. I glance toward Finlay and cower from his unspoken rage. That look is my last warning and I heed it, being careful to keep my eyes to the front of the class and my left elbow tucked against my side.

Class drags on after that, with Finlay's eyes drilling into the side of my head. His glare never leaves me, and his chin never moves. He looks like an emotional statue, with his big, bug-eyes magnetized to my face. Even his friends can't get through to him, and they're doing their best to grab his attention with dumb jokes during our first break.

Luke starts to really pick at him, thinking the way Finlay's treating me is comedic. "Hey, Finlay. What's clear and smells like red paint?"

Finlay doesn't answer.

"Oh, come on, bruh. You know this one."

Finlay continues to scowl toward me, unblinking.

Luke stands and slides up behind my chair so Finlay can see him. "Chloroform," Luke continues, cupping his hand over my mouth like I'm a victim being held hostage by a psychopath. "Shhh," he hushes, when I squirm beneath his firm hand.

I swat at him until he releases me, and scowl while Luke backs away to retake his seat. I fidget beneath Finlay's motionless stare while Luke and his friend burst into laughter. Finlay *is* the psycho-boyfriend Luke jokes about, but mocking Finlay's social awkwardness is only making matters worse for me.

Luke quickly holds his breath when our professor returns to the room. He slaps his friend next to him who continues to laugh. I don't know how much more of this I can take without going off the deep end. I watch the professor head for the door to lock it. Ryan sneaks through the door just in the nick of time. He flashes an intelligent smile at the professor as he passes him and then casually looks my way.

What a shocker. Ryan doesn't return to the seat next to me. Instead, he sits down at the far end of the room a few seats away from Savari—the beautiful blonde girl I once called my best friend. I don't blame Ryan, or her, for that matter. I'd steer clear of me, too. Finlay is a loose cannon, and I feel like we're playing Russian roulette—no one knows when he's going to fire off, not him and especially not me.

I'm embarrassed. Finlay must know that. But he

continues to play his stupid staring game as class resumes, and so I do the only thing in my control. I ignore everyone and everything around me—including Finlay. I scribble in my notebook to make it look like I'm taking a valid interest in the class, but my notes are illegible, and my written words have nothing to do with the garbled noise coming from my professor's mouth, even if I did notice that he's incredibly easy to look at.

I try to concentrate on class but my head won't let me. First, I must punish Finlay for embarrassing me in public. My ignorance is his punishment for acting so selfishly and not trusting my love for him. But what can I do to make him pay? Finlay must pay for this.

My eyes linger on our professor with the obsidian hair. Mr. Varela is one fine specimen—sophistication wrapped in a suit that looks much too expensive for a teacher's salary. It looks like he's actually enjoying himself at the front of the class. I wish Finlay would look at me with that kind of passion. I bet Mr. Varela doesn't disrespect his woman the way Finlay does me.

I'm watching on adoringly when my professor catches my undivided attention. I try not to flinch when he notices the way I'm staring. I have to chew on the inside of my mouth to hang on to my embarrassed smile. I hear his voice hitch in its delivery, and he pauses for a breath, but maybe I'm dreaming. He quickly recovers and looks to the next student.

Finlay isn't so quick to recover from it. It looks like I've found my revenge after all. My eyes glaze over, with Finlay's drilling through the side of my head, again. I know he's just waiting for me to look at him, but I'm not going to do it. I won't give him the satisfaction. I stare straight ahead like he doesn't exist. It's like I don't even exist. There's not another word breathed in class that I hear, embarrassment and anger fueling my mental departure. It's not until I notice students moving around the classroom that I get to my feet, tucking my book against my chest and walking toward Ryan and Savari. I do all of this before Finlay has a second to recover from the shock of me leaving his side.

"Hey, Savari! Wait up." I jog down the stairs and fall into step beside her. A bunch of classmates crowd the stairway behind me. "How've you been? We haven't talked much lately."

She flashes a look toward Finlay, who must be gaining on me by any means necessary. That small look of disgust speaks volumes about how she feels about our dwindling friendship. "No thanks to Finn."

"Please, don't pin this on him. I've been busy." I say it quickly, knowing how much Savari hates when I lie to her. We might not have been friends for long, but we were close, *before*—now, not so much. We cheer for the same team. She's my co-captain of the school's Crimson Squad, but other than that we really are nothing to each other, anymore.

She shakes a full head of straight blonde hair. "Are you sure you're not moving too fast? This guy, you're really in love with him? Because you don't look very happy. You look... different."

Different? What does she know?

"We're in love. There's no reason for us not to be together."

Oh, but there are reasons; if I'd only admit them to myself. I'm living in Finlay's house now. *His house. His rules.* He decides what I buy and when. He decides what I wear and where I go. At first it was innocent—he was protective; it was sweet—but now he decides when I leave the house and who I hang around with. Over the course of the holidays, I managed to alienate all the friends I'd worked so hard to win over since moving to Queens two years ago for school.

Finlay wraps his arm around my waist, pulling me away from the crowd, scowling at Savari in the process. "She's just jealous because she doesn't connect with Luke the way we do," he says against my ear.

The first part is true—she's jealous—but only because we used to be super close. The rest is a line Finlay spoon feeds me daily. It's just one of many things he swamps me with now that he has me under his thumb.

Savari nods at me, disgusted with the woman I've become. "Good to see you, too." Then she walks away with that same sour expression on her face that I've come to recognize all too well.

Luke glances at me with the same disappointment written in his brow but grabs on to Savari's hand to stop her. He tugs her back until they're only a few steps away. Even with him whispering in her ear right next to us, she refuses to look at me.

Luke delivers us a peace offering. "We're all going out tonight and there's room for two more, if you two want." He looks optimistic, squeezing Savari's shoulders.

She's still doing a good job of ignoring me.

Finlay's hugging me tightly against him, seeming to have forgotten about what happened in the classroom, and so I forget about it too. He looks down into my eyes. "What do you think?"

"Maybe we could go out tonight," I say, after I garner enough courage to make the suggestion. We haven't gone out with anyone besides ourselves since the day I moved into his house.

His jaw tightens. Clearly I've read the situation wrong. The beady, black balls in his eyes warn me to reconsider.

"Except we have that thing," I add.

"What thing?" he asks, making me look like a total ass in front of our friends.

I turn my eyes to the floor, and everyone waits for Finlay to end the conversation. "Oh, right. That thing. Yeah, we're busy. Not tonight, I guess," he says to Luke and Savari. "Sorry."

The anger continues to course through his veins, the heat from his body rushing toward me in waves. This argument is not over. Oh, no, it's only just begun. I've learned to keep my mouth shut, speaking only when spoken to—by Finlay. Why can't I just stick to the rules?

Being with Finlay isn't so bad. He loves me. He's not all

bad. He's usually really good to me—usually. The fact of the matter is that everything is fine when we aren't fighting, and I just want us to be happy, like we were before I moved in with him.

The silence on our walk to his car is painful, the grip of his hand cutting off the circulation in mine. I don't bother asking again whether we can go out tonight. Asking dumb questions right now would be a mistake. The ride home is no better, the quietness buzzing like a mosquito stuck in my ear canal. I wait for the show to begin—the Finlay show—wondering when and how it is going to happen this time, praying with basic hope that I'll make it through another night.

4: Survival

F inlay is taking me home for war. I know the drill. Sit there and take it like a woman. Make dinner. Get bitched at for baking it wrong. Clean up the clear glass when he slams the dish of lasagna off the side of the table. Cry on my knees while cleaning the floor, broken like Cinderella but unable to keep a steely face with him standing over me screaming about what a mistake of a human being I am.

"What is wrong with you?" he screams. "Can't you do anything right? All I ask for is an edible plate of food on the table. Is that too much to ask? You can't even get that right."

"I'm sorry, okay?" I cry hysterically. "I'm so fucking sorry."

"You're sorry? You're sorry?"

I zone out after that. Words... they're just words. He doesn't mean it. I've done this to him. This is my fault. If I would have stayed calm, it would have been fine. Maybe if I was a better cook, he wouldn't flip out over everything. He leans toward me to shout in my ear, as if maybe I will hear him better when he's spitting at my ear drum.

I want to scream back at him—tell him to stop—but think better of it, stiffly doing what I know I have to do— bow down and take it. I have to calm the fuck down and get through this, one episode at a time.

I take a deep breath and smear my tears with the sleeve of my shirt. I listen to the seconds tick by, the oversized clock on the wall reminding me that this will all be over soon enough. He starts shouting again, but I can handle it now. This anger will pass, like it always does. He can't keep this up for much longer. The volcano will erupt and soon the sweet, emotional rush will flow again.

I know what Finlay's working toward—make-up sex— but it won't be until I'm a trembling, tear-faced wreck, browbeat into submission. I snap free from that safe place in my mind and tremble from the cold rush of tears on my cheeks. I place the wasted food into a plastic bag Finlay throws at me, together with the broken glass and dirty napkins I used to pick up the saucy mess. A chunk of the broken dish slices across my thumb as it drops into the bag, and I cry out in surprise. Blood instantly pools on the surface of the long cut, and I stare at it, wondering whether it's deep enough to make a bloody mess. It takes a second for Finlay to realize something is wrong.

My eyes fly across the room. Finlay's suddenly watching me with a disgraceful look in his eyes. He notices the drops of blood on the floor and takes a step toward me. I flinch, raising my arm to hide my face, afraid he's finally going to raise a hand on me.

"Please," I beg, not knowing what I beg for anymore. The shouting to stop. The name-calling to end. The rotten feeling inside my soul to subside. *Just hit me and get it over with.*

His hand comes gently down onto my shoulder. "You winced. Why did you wince?" He pauses as the words sink in and make me shudder. "Do you not love me anymore?" He sighs, tears coming to his eyes as I lower my guard. "What a monster I've become." He pours his face into his hands. "Oh, God. What have I done?"

Every second is torture, but this is no show. He means it and I can't escape him. The other Finlay is back, and I can never leave *him*. I drop the bag to the floor, tuck my thumb into the palm of my hand and curl into his crumbling form. The tips of my fingers slide over his wet cheek and drag through his hair. "You know that's not true," I whisper, burying my face into his neck and clutching my injured hand to my chest. "Our love isn't finished yet."

He kisses my wound, tasting my blood before pulling me to the sink. He rinses my hand under a stream of cool water, watching the pink swirling down the drain until the water runs clear. Finlay hands me a paper towel, and I press it against the laceration while he searches the cabinet for peroxide and a bandage. He cleans the fresh wound, dries my hand and covers the sliced skin, kissing the spot now concealed. His eyes remain downturned. Does he feel bad for the way he's treated me? Will he remember this feeling tomorrow? His thumb smooths back and forth over my hand.

"Can you ever forgive me?" he asks, his eyes pleading with the rush of a thousand oceans.

I nod, his lips crashing down upon mine. His kiss is hard and heated, his hands immediately moving to the waistband of my skirt. I pant for air, the need to feel his skin against mine so overwhelming that I throb for him.

"Say yes, Clarisse. I need this," he breathes between harsh kisses, with a heavy hand squeezing my breast. He lifts me onto the table and spreads my legs, pushing against me where I'm most sensitive. "Say yes. Please say yes."

"Yes!" I gasp, when I hear the sound of a key and a jiggling doorknob. He hears it too, but it takes him a second longer to react to it.

"Your mom's home!"

Finlay takes my good hand, tosses the remnants of our argument in the garbage and pulls me into his bedroom, closing the door behind me.

He stalks me toward the bed, and I fall backwards onto it. Sex with Finlay tends to be good, especially after an emotionally-charged argument. Finlay pulls his shirt over his head in a single motion, his pants and underwear shed in the next moment. His eyes are hungry. He's hungry for me, eager to make things right between us, as if sex fixes all things. For him, it often does.

Even though this will be our third time today, it is a moment I look forward to. I shouldn't complain. The sex is still amazing; my body tells me so every time he touches me.

Finlay steals my attention away from the door with an erection so hard it's flattened against his belly. "This is love," he tells me while yanking down my skirt.

His muscles aren't huge, but he's fit, and when he removes the only barrier left between me and him, I see the flex in every agile muscle.

Without checking to see whether I'm even ready for him, he plows into me. I cry out in shock from the invasion. His hands clamp down on my shoulders as the pressure pins me deep into the mattress. I tamp down the bitterness that rises to my throat, feeling repulsed by the way he simply takes it whenever and however he wants it, without protection.

I take steady breaths in and out, matching every other thrust. Just as my body adjusts to the rhythm, he slows down, filling me completely and working himself deeper. He keeps that up, watching my eyes flutter shut and feeling my hips bucking against him, craving the depth he was once giving me.

My body wars with my mind, grinding against him and asking for more while my mind screams for him to stop and roll on a condom. He gets harder, if that is even possible, as my body tightens around him. I scream out, forgetting about the world around me as the sensations spiral from my body like an abstract painting.

He doesn't stop with my orgasm; he only moves faster, slamming into me again and again. My mind resurfaces from my next orgasm, which I realize is not born from love. I clench my teeth down in a mixture of pain too unpleasant to call true pleasure. My body starts to catch up with me, feeling the scrape of all that hardness passing over my sensitized flesh.

"Oww," I cry out as he makes another sharp pass over me. "That hurts, Finn." My whimpering only turns him on more. "No," I gasp, feeling the weight of him bearing down on me.

Tears start to spill out of the corners of my eyes from the rawness as he rams into me long after my second orgasm has expired. I wonder now if the wetness between my legs is tinged red as I sink deeper into my psyche, farther away from the pain and the disgust of being used like a thoughtless ragdoll. I think of the better times—those when I want him. I take him in my hand or rub him just right, until he gives me what I need. He always gives me what I need.

He's good that way: always hard and ready for me. I feel so powerful at times like that, when he succumbs to my sexual prowess. I've started to use sex as a weapon. When I do, Finlay becomes vulnerable. He can't say no to me. Not in the bedroom.

Tonight is not one of those times.

Finlay is not vulnerable and I am not in control. Tonight, I'm using sex as a shield, to protect me from his wrath. Some would call it a coping mechanism. *I call it survival.*

When he's done with me, he finally notices how I've withdrawn, shaking me ruthlessly by the shoulders until I respond to him, his anger threatening to bubble back to the surface. I instantly snap out of it, the soreness between my legs finally registering on a human level.

"Clarisse. Clarisse," he repeats.

"Shhh," I hush him, pressing my index finger into the flesh of his lower lip, now realizing it is fear fueling this rough treatment. "I'm here. I'm okay," I say, running my fingers through his hair. I kiss him and whisper my love, drawing him to my breasts. It's completely innocent and honest, because my love for him is true, and I want nothing more than his love and acceptance—that and for the throbbing pain to stop hurting so damn much.

I ask him to help me clean up and he obeys, taking care of me the only way he knows how. I grab onto him and squeeze my legs around his neck. He clutches onto me like I'm his lifeline in tortured waters. He couldn't escape if he wanted to, but he doesn't and neither does his tongue, which doesn't stop tormenting me until I'm thoroughly fucked and convulsing from the sensory distraction.

It works like a charm, for the both of us. He stakes that claim and hangs it over my head like a noose that I wrap around my own neck. There are a couple of things he and I both know for sure: he owns my body, and if he can't have me, no one can. If he only knew now, the very thing that drives us together would be the thing that digs his selfish ass an early grave.

5: Social Suicide

For once, I had everything going for me: good grades, a full scholarship, popularity. Being a varsity cheerleader has its benefits, but something is missing. Family. Finlay tries to fill that hole for me, for better or for worse. I didn't know that filling that hole would open up new ones, but Savari seems to have set out to remind me of that every chance she gets.

For an entire week, she follows me around and slips in a comment here and a glance there. After class this one time, Finlay needs a bathroom break, leaving Savari a new opportunity to badger me when she catches me lounging on a sofa down the hall. She cranes her neck around, like it's shocking to find me on my own. I shoot her pouty lips, and that makes her smile.

"I don't know why you put up with him, Clarisse. Why do you let him control your life like this? He's bad for your health, and you look like hell."

I don't deny it. I feel like hell, too. There's no doubt in my mind that my life has changed since I've let Finlay Turnbull into it, but I have to admit another thing. "He's nuts, but I love him." And no matter how badly I want to leave him, I can't. There would be no one there to save him from himself, and I honestly believe he will hurt himself without me to balance the bad times with the good.

Savari sighs harshly. "You keep saying that. I'm not sure you understand that what he's showing you is not love. It's possession. There's a difference. It's the difference between a natural, healthy relationship and the one-sided nightmare you're putting yourself through."

I catch Savari flashing a glance down the hall. Finlay quickens his steps when he sees that I have company. Savari smiles in his direction and scurries off but not until she's softly reminded me that I'm not alone. "Later, girl. You know where to find me if you ever need to talk."

Clasping my hands together, I stare down at my linked fingers almost afraid to look up and find out which Finlay I have to deal with now. When I finally do look up, I'm forced to take in the evil stare that bears down upon me.

"Clarisse, what are you doing talking to her?"

My smile flips into my trademark scowl. Does he really think he can control who I talk to? "She's my friend."

"No. No," he snaps, throwing his hands down angrily. "She is not your friend. She tries to put things into your head that aren't there." He leans forward and gets in my face, with passing students starting to stare. "She's trying to break us up. Is that what she was doing just now? Trying to break us up?"

I try to cover his lips with a hushed finger, but he pushes my hand away and drops down onto the couch next to me, slouching forward to bury his face in his hands.

Finlay knows I have cheer practice tonight. He is supposed to be walking me to the gym right now, but this new development poses a problem. I know this isn't something that is going to pass in the next few minutes.

"How am I supposed to let you go now?" he asks me.

I hate when he gets like this, the hysteria apparent in his tone. There's no saying what he'll do or say next. People stare. I cringe. There's no stopping it, and I'm the only one with anything to lose. I don't have time for this right now. I have cheer practice and if I don't distract Finlay and escape this disaster in the next two minutes I'm going to be late. My coach, Kyla the slave-driver, will not have that. Being anything but early is not acceptable in her eyes. If I am late, I will pay for it.

I place my hand on Finlay's thigh and sigh, trying to hide my impatience.

"Don't touch me," he barks. "You've ruined my life. You tell me you love me. You're lying."

I steal my hand back, anger and confusion now mingling with his accusations. "Stop it. Don't say that. You know that's not true."

He looks up at me with a painful glance and dry, pouted

lips. "Then why can't you say it."

"I love you," I state firmly.

He shakes his head and turns his pout to the floor, closing his eyes in the process. "You can't even say it and mean it, anymore. What did she say to you?" He huffs, like he just figured it all out. "I can't believe you're leaving me."

"I'm not leaving you," I say, slumping into myself. "I just want to go to practice."

He grits his teeth, and it looks like his head might explode soon if he doesn't take a breath. "You're choosing them over me. You want me to be alone. Is that it?"

I whimper, too embarrassed to let the passing students see me cry, but too frustrated by all this crazy talk to relate to him. "Finlay, you're not making any sense."

He's shaking his head again, like there's a voice inside it telling him horrible things I can't hear. "I can't believe you're doing this to me. After everything I've done for you."

Again, there it is. Like every time we argue. He plays the provider card, bringing up the fact that I moved into his house, and his mother pays the utility bills. He never admits who buys all the groceries or who does all the cleaning or cooks all the meals. That's because the answer doesn't help his situation. He wants to act like he has control over our entire relationship, and I can't take it much longer. He has to know this is not helping us.

Our discussion takes longer than planned, and I end it with, "I'll see you tonight, okay?" I don't know how I finally make it to practice, but it's without an answer from Finlay. At least he left the foyer, though, so I'm free to change and race my ass to the gym.

When I skip into the west entrance, I'm late, and I know Coach Kyla will make a point of punishing me in front of my entire team for it. I watch her lay out two small pylons while I finish my warmup. I join up with the rest of the Crimson squad and smile, even though it's the last thing I feel like doing

"You're late." Coach Kyla points to the red line taped on the floor. "Line up, Blackwell."

I jog over and stand next to the small orange pylon, with the entire team watching. A few girls follow me over mistakenly.

"No, not you," Coach Kyla says pointedly. "Clarisse will be the only one running suicides for us tonight."

Great. Suicides. My favorite. "How many?" I ask, knowing I'm not going to like the answer.

"Keep going until I tell you to stop."

I nod, outwardly smiling while internally cringing, and start as soon as she clicks on her stopwatch. I sprint across the room and touch the small pylon, pushing my toe into the floor and turning back in the opposite direction.

"Faster!" she shouts.

I dig in deep and push harder. After six more passes back and forth, I slow to a jog, my breaths now ragged and clipped.

"Not fast enough," Coach Kyla snaps, staring at the stopwatch while the rest of my team watches the show.

Minutes later, my legs feel like rubber, and when I reach out to touch the pylon, I nearly miss it and crash onto the floor, but I don't stop. I stumble, but I keep going. I keep pushing harder. My thighs burn, and my lungs are on fire, but I won't give up.

When Coach Kyla finally thinks she's made her point, I dive onto the floor and lie there in an attempt to catch my breath while she stands over me warning everyone else not to make the same mistake as I did.

"You see? No one is indispensable on this team, not even the captain."

What a slap in the face—a reminder that it may have taken two years to earn my title, but it can be taken away just like that. I know I can't be pulling shit like this and expect things to go down any other way. Everything I do is scrutinized as it is. With the title of Captain, there comes certain responsibility. I am accountable to my team. We all have to be on our best behavior, with or without our cheerleading uniforms on. These girls look up to me, and I can't let them down.

"Blackwell," Coach Kyla reminds me in a stale tone, "If you aren't in a good place right now, fake it."

I want to roll my eyes and walk away, but Coach Kyla's voice echoes through the gym, announcing my problems to the entire squad.

"Everyone on the wall!" she shouts "Wall sits starting in five... four..."

I get up to one knee and stumble toward the nearest wall, slamming my back against it.

"Three... two... one... and sit."

I bend my knees and sit against the wall, like everyone else, my thighs trembling the second I sink into the squat. This cheerleading business is no joke. Just to associate yourself with our squad puts you higher on the social ladder. The standards are raised for those on the team and so are expectations.

I cry out and it helps ease the pain. It takes everything in me to keep going. Years of determination, sweat, blood, and tears come together and get me through. Plain old hard work and dedication isn't enough anymore. To show weakness—to give up when things are looking bleak—is to alienate yourself from the squad. It's social suicide.

My thighs jump unnaturally, but I suck it up and sink deeper into my psyche, the only place where I can find peace in this cracked world.

Image is everything, and that is one thing Finlay can't ever control. I won't let him.

6: Reckless Behavior

Our three hour practice really kicks my ass, the emotional turmoil from earlier coming rushing back to me. I walk to Finlay's car alone, and I can't even paste on a fake smile anymore. It's a night like any other night, except it's not any other night. I'm locked and loaded, just waiting for someone to push me over the edge. It won't take much.

I dip into the driver's seat, my frown deepening while I contemplate my options. I hug the steering wheel, knowing I'm barely skating on the edge of a mental breakdown. I should call someone. But who would I call?

Savari hasn't shown much interest in me lately. Unless it involves me leaving Finlay, she wants no part in it. Then there's Finlay. I'm driving his car, so it's not like he can come and get me. Besides, he's the last person I want to call right now. I huff in misery, because there really is no one else. I have no one. I moved to New York to forget—forget about everything that happened and move on from my horrible past.

I had hoped to slip into the fast-paced lifestyle and earn an Ivy League education with a smile on my face, but the truth is I have no real reason to smile. When my parents died, they left me nothing. Not unless you consider collection agencies your friend. I spent my last few dollars on a fancy outfit, cashed out every last dollar on their credit cards to fund my world-class education, and skipped town.

It seemed like a good idea at the time, and it even worked for a while, but what do I have to show for it? A class schedule that completely ruins me and the depressing realization that I am alone again. No amount of therapy will ever be enough. My parents are dead. I cannot fix that. Finlay is the closest thing I have to family now. That's a scary realization.

I cry into the steering wheel and consider whether anyone would even care if I took my own life. How would I even do it? I consider stepping on the gas and slamming into a tree. It seems a bit of a crap shoot. Then I think about the gun Finlay hides under his nightstand. It could work. But what about Finlay? And what about me? Knowing my luck, I'd probably end up in a hospital, paralyzed, where my parents' creditors learn about my real identity and finally catch up with me.

With tearful eyes, I start the car and throw it into reverse. I swipe the wetness fiercely from my cheeks and stomp on the gas pedal, not much caring whether I hit the car behind me. My life is in shambles. I'm beyond miserable, coming undone. What am I going to do?

Horrible ideas plague me on the entire ride home, my eyes forgetting all the rules of the road. I finally come to where I'm a block away from home—*his* home. I swipe away more tears, but my eyes fill right back up with them.

I want to say that no one controls me but me. I would be lying. I know now that death is the only way I'll ever be in control again. Finlay wouldn't have it any other way. I pull into the small driveway and stare into space, enveloped by the darkness of the night and my deepest thoughts. Even if I want to, I can't leave. He'll never let me go. As long as Finlay lives, I will be forever his.

I sit in the driveway for a long time, sobbing, contemplating whether it's worth the fight anymore, wondering how I'm going to deal with him tonight. My head cannot handle another episode. I'm not sure how much of any of this I can take before I snap completely, beyond repair.

I sling my heavy sport bag over my shoulder and toss my keys into it. When I finally pull open the car door, I see Finlay has joined me. He's standing mere steps away and emerges from the shadows around the house. How long has he been standing there? Does he know how volatile my thoughts are right now?

He steps toward me, and I hold my breath, my muscles jumping with exhaustion.

"I'm so sorry," he cries, pulling me against his chest.

We cry together, and I squeeze onto him tightly, relieved that he's repenting. Everything is going to be okay now. I just know it. He kisses me, and everything snaps back into place.

His hands start to roam around my body. "Let's go inside." He takes the strap of my sports bag over his shoulder and slips his other hand in mine, pulling me inside the house and taking me to our room without detouring.

He pushes me back onto the bed and stares down at me. I worry about the crazed look in his eyes. The love and regret I'd seen in his eyes outside has diminished and has been replaced with pure, animalistic need. He always works to please me, and most nights he does, but tonight would not be one of them.

Finlay recklessly tugs my shirt over my head, snagging it on my earring. I try not to whimper, knowing it will piss him off, while I secretly check my ear expecting to find blood. Before I can tell whether my earring is still intact, I place my hand at my side because Finlay clearly doesn't like how I'm responding to his violence. He monitors my every move, and I will be punished if I don't get my act together.

When I relent, his mouth comes down on mine. His kiss is jagged and demanding, his mouth feeding from me like a starved bird. It's nothing like the apology he'd given me in the driveway, but I accept it with an open heart, hoping that the apologetic, caring Finlay will come back to me. That's the only problem: I never know which lover I'm going to get.

I don't like this one.

Tonight, he's exceptionally rough with me, and I never like the feeling of being completely dominated by him—especially when my surrender is forced for his pleasure. First, he rips my underwear as he takes them down, sniffing them deeply before tucking them into his front pocket. Before he even unzips his pants, I can see how hard this is making him. When he yanks down his pants, his erection is confirmation of my suspicions. He leans over me, grabs onto my shoulder and takes what is his with a swift lunge.

His forearm digs into my chest with the weight of his body ripping the air from my lungs. It's at times like this I'm afraid he's actually trying to suffocate me. Lately, it seems that the only time he is fully satisfied is when he has complete control over *my everything*—even the air that I breathe. I lie there limply, hiding beneath my last shred of sanity while he thrusts into me without any protection or lubrication, destroying every fibre of my independence with each agonizing motion.

It takes everything in me to whimper softly and not let it sound like I'm in pain. I want to cry as oxygen just barely screams past my throat. His arm slides toward my neck and digs into my skin, until it feels like he's severing my head from my body. I gasp for air, and it only makes him press harder and faster. The weight of his body has me pinned to the bed. I squirm beneath him as my body struggles to function without a breath.

I want to say stop, but I can't get the words to reach my lips. My arms thrash at my sides, but nothing I do lessens the blow. I kick and flail until I steal a sharp breath.

"Lie still," Finlay barks. "I'm almost there."

A cry finally reaches my mouth, and it howls through the room. I think I can make it. He's almost done. If I just hang on for one minute more. But my body aches with a rawness I bury deep within my psyche, in a place I care never to remember. Tears stream down my face and land at the valley in my neck where his thumb is now pressing. There will be bruises. The marks are becoming more and more difficult to hide.

"Just like that," he says, as if I don't already feel degraded enough as it is.

I try not to shudder, knowing it'll only take longer if I show any hint of the disgust I feel in my racing heart. I can get through this. It'll be over any second now. I just have to push through the pain. I'll be okay, just as soon as he's through.

Pain screams through my lungs the longer they're starved for air. My head gets light, the backs of my eyes pulling tightly like they're connected to my body by strings. I sink deeper into my subconscious, settling into that familiar *just barely coping* state, like I have on the two other occasions when I let him go this far.

I struggle to find my relaxed state. Blank white walls. Nice calm beach. Sweet new love. I grasp on to any memory that will steal me from this traumatizing experience. I remember how amazing it had been that first time—our first time. He was so gentle and cautious. He did everything to make sure I was okay and enjoying myself, and I was. Now, I am not—close to suffocating and far from reality.

I like feeling cherished like many women do. I love how Finlay knows how to read me, figures out what I want and gives it to me right when I need it. Right now, I need air. My eyelashes wearily flutter open. I plead with him to finish. Beady black eyes burn into mine, but my look is surely vacant as he finds a violent release.

His lips come down on my mine as I choke for a breath. He steals the last of my oxygen, backs away and smiles, taking my steady composure with him.

I can't breathe!

I roll to a sitting position and gasp repeatedly, with my hands clutching my throat.

Finlay is very pleased with himself. The grin he's wearing when the stars in my vision subside enough for me to see him disgusts me.

The man I love is completely taken by the way he hurts me. It's like a drug that feeds his mental illness at times when he's unsure of himself. It's not healthy for him, and it's life-threatening for me.

"That was good, baby," he tells me, as if I should agree with him while choking for a basic necessity.

I want to drop to the floor onto my knees and beg for him to stop this. I need this to stop. But he can see right through me. He knows exactly what I'm thinking. Normally, that would piss him off, but something has him acting strange tonight.

The scowl crosses over my eyes before I can even stop it.

He used my body like a dummy, and I let him. Why do I let him? With a ragged breath I swipe away the tears. I flip the blankets off my body and swing my legs off the side of the bed, listening inquisitively to Finlay's pleased laugh as I stand up and squint at the flood of warmth running down my legs.

"Ugh!" I whimper, alarmed by the volume of liquid absorbing into the carpet at my feet.

I panic, having no idea what the fuck he's laughing at, wishing I could slap that selfish look right off his face and ask him to help me fix this.

"What is it?" I say, trying to think clearly. The bedsheets appear to be as soaked as my thighs. Something is very wrong here. My eyes connect with Finlay's. He's still grinning smugly, while I'm getting more worked up by the second.

My first thought is blood. I leap away from the bed and stare down at myself and then at the bed. Finlay's outright laughing now. The more I stress about what's happening, the harder he laughs.

"What—" I gasp.

"When you gotta go, you gotta go."

The smell finally hits me as I put it all together. "You fucking disgusting prick!" I feel so degraded and dirty. I have never felt this filthy in all my twenty-one years. "I fucking hate you."

In a fit of tears, I cover my body with the urine soaked sheet and run to the bathroom, curling up into a ball on the floor and drowning myself in tears of betrayal and disrespect.

7: Permanent Footprints

T he bathroom is the only place I feel safe, but the floor tiles give me a chill, so I force myself to stop wallowing in my filth. I reach for the door handle and secure the lock before crawling to the tub. I run the water through my fingers until it's scalding hot and then pull on the shower and scrub myself free of Finlay's disrespect. No matter how hard I scrub, and no matter how hard I cry, I feel like I will never be able to rid myself of the insult.

When I hear a small knock at the door, I pray it's not him. "Yes?" I ask, hoping his mother's finally come to her senses and has come to check on me. With no answer, though, I know it's him, and he takes my *yes* as an offer for him to come in.

Hot water continues to prickle my skin as Finlay picks the lock in silence and enters the room. I fight back angry tears, searching for a weapon but coming up with only a bottle of shampoo. I peer around the edge of the shower curtain, without pulling it aside. That's when I see him. Finlay's upset, warring with himself and mouthing things toward the floor. He notices me watching him and whips the shower curtain open. I'm suddenly scared again, but my anger returns, too.

Still clutching the shampoo bottle, I curse at him. "Stay the fuck away from me."

But he doesn't listen. He's stripping off his underwear and shaking his head. As soon as his underwear lands on the floor, he steps into the shower with me, invading this one small place I thought was my safe haven. I choke back the tears. He doesn't deserve them.

"Move over," he orders, taking up the better half of the shower.

He stands under the stream of water and tells me to close the curtain. I refuse to listen. I glare at him through irritated eyes. I want to tell him to get out. I want to tell him to leave me the fuck alone. I want to tell him to get a fucking life.

But I can't.

I put down the shampoo bottle and close my eyes, jumping when Finlay shouts at me.

"Close it!"

I blindly listen, swiping the curtain shut. He nods toward the soap. I hand it to him but try to keep my distance. I can't let him touch me. I know exactly what he's doing as he lathers the bar of soap between his palms.

"You can't stay mad," he insists, rolling a soapy hand over my breast and squeezing it gently.

I close my eyes, torn between the shame and desire now blooming low in my belly.

"I'm sorry, Clarisse."

My eyes flash forward. He doesn't look sorry. His body is rather erect, like this game of cat and mouse is the ultimate thrill for him.

Finlay licks his lips and strokes my breasts again. "Come here." His lips hook onto mine as he continues to massage a swollen breast with the bar of soap pressed between his palm and my wet skin.

I bite his lip, drawing blood. He smiles because he likes it. His hand slides slowly down my body, leaving a foaming trail down my middle, until he's stroking me at the juncture between my thighs. My body defies me, warming to his touch and craving more of his affection. This is a new low for me.

What am I supposed to do? My mind is telling me to chop it off, but my body is begging him to make better use of it. I know this is not healthy. I know in my heart that a man would not do this to the woman he loves. But I also know what he would do if I were to ever leave him. I could never live with myself if that happened.

Finlay holds on to a very erect penis and gives it a stroke, licking his full bottom lip in the process. He pushes against me, making me step backwards until I'm flattened against the cold wall of the shower. He presses it between my thighs, sliding through the soapy softness.

"Let me in." He looks down at me like he's the big, bad wolf and I'm a vulnerable little piggy.

"Fuck you," I rasp, glaring into lust-filled eyes.

He loves the chase even more than the finale, and I don't like the way he makes my body ache for the very thing that causes a lot of my pain.

"This isn't right."

"Clarisse," he hisses, sliding against me. "You know I didn't mean to hurt you. It was no big deal. I know you want this. Let me make it better." He pulls back and pushes forward again, the pressure of his stiffness making me tighten with anticipation. "We're just fine. This is okay," he says, playing the part of the little devil on my shoulder.

I try to stifle the tears that prick the back of my eyes, knowing what seeing them will do to him. I hate fighting, but my independence orders me to punish him for this even while my body argues the matter.

"You want this, Clarisse. You do, baby." He plunges between my thighs again, burying his soapy dick in my softness.

"No!" I screech, wanting to stop myself from giving in to him, wondering if someone will come to my rescue if I shout loud enough.

No one responds. There's no knock on the door. Once the echo of my voice subsides, so does the threat of tears. Finlay drags away the hair where it's fallen into my eyes and sprinkles my eyelids with kisses, one at a time. He draws soapy circles down my body, spiraling toward my crotch, where I let him touch me.

He knows how to handle me, relying on the soft texture of the soap to gain entry, first with his fingers and then with the most rigid muscle on his body.

"See?" he says. "You like it. Your body doesn't lie."

I whimper from the sensitivity when he slides in deep, partly from lust and partly from the knowledge that I will never feel completely safe with him again.

He continues to enter my body, with practiced motions,

and my body forgives his deception meeting every thrust. "See that, Clarisse. You *do* want me."

"No," I answer, but he keeps going, my own body responding to him, defying my spoken words.

"Yes," he repeats, with a solid, slippery shaft proving it.

I keep opposing a fight I am bound to lose. He smirks into my eyes, slowly entering me and pressing me into the shower wall.

"No," I say.

My body may be enjoying this, but my heart dearly wants him to stop. It's like he knows this and deliberately takes his time, kissing me like he hasn't just ruined me for all men. His tongue is soft and sweet, but I will not feel guilty for how I've treated him. I whimper from the depth of his thrusts, but not because it physically hurts. He answers my natural plea and moves faster, driving me into the wall, with gritted teeth and brut determination.

"No," I repeat, not wanting him to finish me. "No," I huff, feeling my body winding up for a cosmic end. Every time he drives into me, I cry out. "No. No. No," screaming when I find my release.

Finlay's lips seal over mine, and his tongue sweeps into my mouth, just as my body shatters from the most outrageous orgasm.

He thrusts into me again as I let go, giving in to the storm of sensations and emotion. He finishes too, gazing into my eyes as I sink to my knees, soaking up my moment of weakness and feeding on his power over me. Satisfaction radiates from his expression like an all-consuming darkness, as he pecks my cheek and leaves the shower soaking wet.

8: Imprisoned

I attend school the next day, lost in a blur of dependence and unspoken insults, the captain of the varsity cheer squad and a complete prisoner in my own home. In the quiet of my own mind, I make a few decisions. This is not who I am. This is not who I aspire to be. Where is the independent woman I was when I started this journey? I will find her, if it is the last thing I do.

After the hell Coach Kyla put me through the other night, I half expected her to test me again. Instead, she lightens up and sends us all home from practice a few minutes early. I take those few extra minutes and cruise home, contemplating life. I pull into the driveway and stare at the house. Just because all the lights are off doesn't mean nobody's home. I scour the shadows, but no monsters appear, so I rush to the door, yank off my shoes, and sweep into the bedroom, surprised but relieved to find it empty too.

Believing this might be my only chance, I begin to frantically throw my undergarments into my bag together with a few toiletries. Killing myself is not the answer, but at the rate Finlay's been escalating, I fear he's going to turn violent one of these times and make that decision for me. I see the way his anger takes over, and it's not the first time I've feared for my life. I don't plan on hanging around to find out whether he can push that boundary with me again.

As soon as I throw a few items of clothes together, I turn for the door. It's like I almost expect Finlay to be standing there with his gun. That thought gets me hurrying faster. I race to the door, again rather surprised that I've made it to my shoes without a gun being waved in my face. I slowly turn the knob and exhale, preparing to make a run for it. If I could only get to the street, I would be free.

Where will I go? One step at a time. When I step outside, darkness envelopes me. It has to be past nine, which makes me wonder where I'll find Finlay or, worse yet, where he'll find me. I fumble with a handful of keys, squinting to find the one to lock the deadbolt.

"Going somewhere?" His voice is as dark as the night.

I see a shadow standing there, backlit by the light I'd left on in the bedroom. All I see is a silhouette of his body, holding a bow and arrow pointed directly at me. He's going to kill me, and there's nothing I can do about it. I drop my bag on the ground and hold out my hands, palms faced out. If I run, he will find me and take me back to this hell I call life. I'd rather he just end it here and now.

Finlay kicks something hard, and it lands next to my feet. Before I can even take a breath, three arrows slice into the object. The neighbor's Golden Retriever bounds toward me and attacks the flattened basketball. Out of habit and alarm, I squat to pet the poor dog, thankful she is too old to beat the ball to the ground. When I stand up, Finlay's there lifting my bag back onto my shoulder.

"You really thought I'd shoot you?" I can hear the dark emotion thick in his voice. I've offended him deeply. There is redness in and around his eyes. He's been crying again—struggling with the monsters inside his head. "I'd never hurt you, Clarisse."

I used to believe that, but he's already done irreparable harm. Tears begin to sting my eyes and soon roll down my cheeks. My heart screams for me to get the hell out of here, knowing full well that I will never be free of this man. I can't leave. I know this now.

"If you want to go, go," he says. "I'm sure your boyfriend will be happy to see I'm finally out of the picture."

"There is no boyfriend, Finlay. You're the only man in my life," I tell him, because it's true and because no matter how badly I need to leave I don't want him to hurt himself.

The lies I've told in my lifetime work against me, but he can't possibly know the truth. It's clear, though, he doesn't believe a word I say, his fingers gliding up the bowstring and pulling it back with an arrow pointed straight at my chest.

Feeling threatened, but with acceptance, I close my eyes and wait for whatever fate he deals me. "I love you," I cry softly, "but I can't live like this anymore. I have to leave."

The friendly dog licks my palm and, sensing my pain, whines into the night. Finlay lunges forward and kicks the flattened ball, knowing what will happen next. Without fear or logic, the dog chases after the ball.

"No!" I scream, as another arrow stabs into the ball.

Finlay speaks with vulgarity evident in his tone. "You don't like it here? Leave. But know that it'll be my blood on your hands if you do." He turns away but his voice doesn't soften. "Have fun explaining to my mom how selfish you are—taking my heart. I can't live without you, Clarisse."

My stomach retches with anxiety. I now fear not only for the dog's safety, but for Finlay's and my own. "Don't say that. Yes, you can."

He shakes his head with certainty. "If you leave, Clarisse, I'm a dead man. I'll sink these arrows right into my chest. You might as well do it right here, right now. That's what it feels like to know you're leaving me."

"Finlay, no. You can't do that. But I can't keep doing this. I can't take it anymore."

"I will do it. You know I will." He holds the arrows in front of his chest and presses the heads into the fabric of his hoodie.

"Don't do it. Please," I beg. "I could never live with myself."

He closes his eyes and tears pinch out. "If you don't love me, I have no reason to live."

"Stop it!" I shriek. "I love you so fucking much. I don't want you to do it and you said you'd never hurt me."

"This won't hurt you one bit, Clarisse. I promise."

I shake my head furiously. "Don't you see? By doing this you are hurting me!" I'll say anything to stop him from harming himself at this point. I've already lost two people in my life to mental illness; I doubt I could survive another mishap. "I love you."

Emotion creeps back into Finlay's voice. "You love me?"

Even though I know I need to leave this relationship, I do love him with all that I have. "I do."

He throws down the arrow and captures me against his chest as he sobs into my neck. "I'll never leave you."

I wrap my arms around him, as he leans the bow against his leg. He hugs me tightly.

"I never want to lose you, Clarisse. I love you more than life itself."

And I believe him. "I know you do, baby," I say, melting against his hot body. "I'm so sorry for tonight." The words are rushing out of my mouth before I can even think to stall them.

"I'm sorry, too. I don't know what I was thinking."

I sigh with relief. The neighbor's elderly dog would be safe another day. It paws at the gate and lets itself out of the backyard. We return inside the house and make our way to Finlay's bedroom. I quickly dress the bed with clean sheets and flop back onto it. Finlay crawls over top of me, his body so lean and stiff. After the rush of emotions, I expect he wants to feel a connection with me that can only be fused by one thing.

"I need you," I whisper, thinking it's what he wants to hear. The way he presses against me, it's hard to believe he's leaning toward anything else, but he kisses me once and rolls aside.

"Not tonight."

Confusion cripples me. I lie there stiffly, lost in a pool of my own anxieties. He doesn't want me, but he won't let me go. I can't leave him. If I do, he'll kill himself and I'll be dead inside. I have to accept that we are a pair. He is made for me, as I am for him.

I stare at the shadows on the ceiling and then close my tear-filled eyes. This is my life now.

9: A Real Goodbye

By the March break, my grades have taken a nose dive. It must be the first night I've not cried in weeks, which only leaves me worried about the shit I'll have to take when I get home. Finlay knows the basketball team has a big away game tomorrow and I absolutely cannot miss it. I've been working my ass off for this one, and I'm going to be there no matter what. He knows this.

I make it to practice without a fight for a change. I take the bus home and get there by nine thirty, scarf down a few crackers, and chase it with a bottle of water. I tiptoe past his mother in the living room, sneak into my bedroom, drop my pants to the floor, and slip into bed.

The fact that Finlay's already dimmed the lights and drawn the covers up to his chest makes me nervous. I don't turn on the light, because I don't want to wake him if he's legitimately sleeping, but who am I kidding? He's not asleep. He's surely stewing, just waiting for me to say something to set him off.

I fight the tightness in my chest and force steady breaths. I imagine the sun and sand and a nice calm beach—anything to help me fall asleep and avoid the fallout that happens every time there's an away game. I pull the covers to my chin and close my eyes, drifting off into a restless sleep. As uneasiness settles over me, crazy dreams wrack my brain. Something bad is going to happen. I just know it.

Saturday morning comes slowly, and I awaken to an empty bed. I'm not at all shocked when I find the covers pulled firmly over the pillows next to me. I glance at the alarm clock mere minutes before it's due to go off and quickly shuffle across the room to shut it off, wearing a T-shirt that just barely covers my butt. I allow myself to take a deep, relaxing breath. The calm will be short-lived.

Without seeing Finlay's face or hearing his voice, I can tell this morning is going to be a trying one. Although it's silent and I haven't laid eyes on him yet, I can sense the way anxiety rolls off him from across the house. I enjoy the last moment to myself, packing my things for this weekend's trip before all hell breaks loose.

I tiptoe through the sitting room and let myself into the dark bathroom before Finlay realizes I've even awakened. I turn the lock on the silver handle and flick on the light. I'm not in the mood for a conjugal visit, and I know if I don't lock the door that's exactly what I'll get. Although that's not stopped him before, I'm not about to make it easy for him. I yank open the shower curtain and, with a twist of a handle, hot water rushes from the shower head.

I strip off my shirt, test the water, and hop in. By the time I've soaked my hair with water, I hear Finlay jiggling the door handle. I know I'll pay for locking the door later, but I can get past this. The bus leaves the school in an hour. I have little time to spare for fighting.

With towel-dried hair, wearing a short, black robe, I pad toward the kitchen. Our eyes connect like magnets, but I don't move toward him. I go straight for the cupboard and pull a spoon from the drawer. When I shake my cereal into my bowl, it cuts the silence like the gunfire that starts a race. Ignoring the chill in the air, I grab the milk, fill my bowl until my cereal's floating, and then return it to the fridge.

As my chair screeches across the kitchen floor, still, no one speaks. Finlay leaves me to eat in peace. Well, sort of. He sits in the chair across from me, brooding. I can see the words boiling inside. I eat quickly, waiting for an explosion that doesn't happen.

When I drop my dish into the sink, Finlay gets to his feet. He follows me to the bedroom and watches me closely, as I dress and run a brush through my hair. I pull my hair into a high ponytail, shove my costume into the top of my sports bag, and strap it over my shoulder. I smile at him softly, but I don't get a response. Losing the smile, I leave the room and make my way across the house. Again, he follows me nimbly, like a mute stalker. We both pull our shoes on, and he walks me outside.

"So, are you planning on ignoring me all morning?" He's livid. "I'm not going to see you all weekend and you're avoiding me? How do you think that makes me feel, you being shady like that? Is there something you'd like to tell me?"

I sigh, thinking about how close I was to getting out of here on time for a change. I guess taking the bus is out of the question now. "It's nothing, Finlay. I'm just tired. I had a long day yesterday and didn't sleep well last night."

"That's funny; you didn't say anything about having a hard day when you got home so late last night."

"Late? I was home by nine thirty. Practice ran a little longer than normal. You were asleep when I got home and I didn't want to wake you."

"That's bullshit and you know it," he snaps, flashing his teeth. "It's Ryan, isn't it? You're seeing him behind my back. You somehow think that twenty minutes here or there will go unnoticed?"

He acts like this conversation is new, like he doesn't bring it up every time I'm due to go away. It's only the five hundredth time he's accused me of cheating on him, more particularly with Ryan, the blond basketball captain. Even though I find Ryan attractive—everyone does—he has a girlfriend and I'm unavailable. I would never cheat on Finlay. I've been nothing but faithful to him.

Finlay pulls open the driver side door of his car and gets into the front seat. I already know if I don't go along with him, I'm guaranteed to be late. I pile into the passenger seat with my bag as quickly as I can, but I can't leave his accusation alone.

"That is ridiculous. You know I'm not cheating on you. I would never do that to you."

As he pulls out of the driveway, he glances at me. "Are you sure about that?"

"Yes!" My answer is most certain, while my brain spins with uncertainty about leaving him like this. "I told you. Practice ran late. I came straight home."

"You came straight home," he repeats.

"I promise you!'

The more we argue, the deeper his foot presses into the accelerator. I try to focus on a passing tree but fail to.

"You're telling me you don't want to fuck Ryan and all his roid-infested teammates?"

"Finlay," I moan.

"I find that hard to believe. I see the way you look at them when they're out on the court." He shifts gears, with his voice loud, harsh, and hurtful. If he doesn't calm down, he's bound to take out a pole. "Ryan especially," he adds, barely scraping by the next yellow light.

I refuse to show him how much it affects me every time we fight like this. He has to know how this hurts. "That's an asshole thing to say."

"But you're not answering me."

"Fuck you. How's that for an answer?"

"So you do want him."

"Finlay, are you kidding me right now? Are you seriously doing this to me, now?"

He's pulling down the long driveway toward the school, and we're in a full on shouting match. I know if we don't resolve this in the next five seconds, the whole fucking basketball team is going to see what a train wreck I am.

He weaves around the car in front of us and slams his brakes, just as a police officer lifts his hand to bring us to a stop. The tires skid across the pavement, leaving the car jolting backward mere inches from the man's hand. The cop strides toward the car as Finlay opens his window.

"What's the hurry?" The officer looks seriously curious to know what has Finlay driving like a maniac. The cop looks across the dashboard to me with raised eyebrows, like I might have a better answer for him.

"My girlfriend is running a little late."

He looks back at Finlay with a hard frown pressed into his mouth. "Maybe next time you should leave yourself a little extra time, right?"

The officer glances at me again. I cup my elbow and hide

the black rings under my eyes with my opposite hand. He can tell we've been fighting.

"Slow down," he says, leaving Finlay with a gentle warning.

I blow out a breath as Finlay slowly pulls back into traffic. He quickly resumes his speed and turns toward me.

"Are you?"

"Am I what?"

"Sleeping with him." He's seriously unsure whether or not I'm faithful. How can this be a topic of conversation every freaking time I leave his side?

"Finlay, you know I love you. You're the only man in my life. Ryan is not even on my radar. You have my heart."

As Finlay pulls up to the curb, I lift my bag onto my lap. "I'm leaving now and you need to trust me. Do you think you can do that?"

His eyes dart down the sidewalk where he finds the last of the basketball team boarding the bus. Ryan must already be on board. Thank God.

"Maybe I should come, too." He's that unsure about me, and his insecurities drive his scary, stalker image to another level.

"No. I have to do this on my own. You can't be following me around and driving across the country. What about your work? You have to trust me, Finlay. I've not done anything to make you not trust me."

I reach for my door handle, but he hits the lock button, trapping me inside the car. With a deep breath, I turn toward him. "You have to let me go."

Finlay watches the way my coach waves for me to hurry and how a couple guys on the basketball team have stopped at the back of the bus to stare. Finlay squeezes onto my hand where no one can see but me. I stare at our entwined fingers. The silence has to end.

"I'm going. I have to go," I say. "I've made this promise to my team. They need me."

"No, I need you. I need you, Clarisse."

His grip slides down to my wrist, and he shows me a pair

of handcuffs that materialize from his pocket. Is he going to forcibly keep me in the car? I fear that he will, but he glances toward the school with regret flickering in his steely eyes. Then he turns back to me.

"I don't want you to go."

I'm ready to have a panic attack. I want to scream. I'm going to cry. I swallow it back, but it's hard.

"I've thought of ways I could stop you from going." He flashes me the cuffs and sadness pours from that wicked smile.

I look directly into his eyes, hating the wounded look on his face as I explain, "I have to go. We've discussed this before. I'm going, Finlay. Let me go."

I mean it, both literally and metaphorically, but he still doesn't release my wrist.

"Finlay, please."

He doesn't want me to go, but this is important to me. I've worked so hard for this. I earned a scholarship that already has a caution tagged onto it thanks to my terrible GPA. If I don't get my act together, I'll be cut from the team and dropped from the program. I need to get back to where I was a year ago and earn my life back.

I turn my eyes to the bus. My coach is looking pissed as she glances at me and then to her phone.

It's time for me to man up.

I press the unlock button and open my door.

Finlay catches onto my wrist with his other hand and speaks with hostility. "This is a defining moment in our relationship and you're just going to walk away?"

I notice how everyone has long ago boarded one of the two buses, and the first one is already pulling away. Coach Kyla is the only one standing by the door of the second bus, staring Finlay down with narrowed eyes. He's now fidgeting with the handcuffs, and I'm afraid that he might slap them on me yet.

With a sigh, I finally take a stand. "We will have to talk about this later. This is a responsibility I'm not going to skip out on. I have to go now."

I feel overwhelmed by the pressure, but my impatience pulls through long enough for Finlay to loosen his grip enough for me to pull away from him.

"Don't I at least get a kiss?" he mocks, as I go to close the door between us. "Or am I not good enough for you anymore?"

I fear that the worst hasn't passed yet and glare at him to make my point as I lean across the front seat. "Quit it. I love you," I say before we share a kiss that feels like a cold goodbye.

His actions speak volumes. If tension were a visible thing, the car would have been filled to the brim with it. I pull my sports bag out of the car, place the strap on my shoulder, and run to the bus without turning back. I can feel Finlay's eyes burning into my back, like a warning echoing through my body, but I ignore it.

"It's nice to know where I stand," Finlay shouts after me, taking his final stab.

He turns his head and his car squeals away, knowing how much I hate it when he drives like a crazy person. I hear him grinding gears as he tries to skip a few. I'm not the only one who notices. I close my eyes and try to act unaffected by his childish act, but the truth is, I'm falling apart inside. Coach Kyla leaves it alone for the moment. If she hadn't, I'm afraid it would have been a little too much.

When I finally climb onto the bus, my coach follows me up the stairs. "It's about time you join us, Blackwell," she says quietly. It looks like I'm spared a lecture this time.

No one else speaks to me right away. They must see it in my eyes that I can't handle it right now. We have a six-hour drive ahead of us, and I use the first half of the ride to piece myself back together. Earbuds make it easy for me to sink into my seat and avoid the rest of the team, but I know there will be questions later—questions I'm not sure I'm prepared to answer yet.

After making good use of the food stop, I rejoin the team on the bus. My girls take the seats right in front of me while I catch my first real breath. I can stop checking over my shoulders now. It looks like Finlay has not followed me, and the bus is speeding down the highway again. I spin around to see who's sitting behind me and find relief in the knowledge that Ryan is out of earshot. Not that Finlay would know that, but I don't think I could deal with Ryan's wit, charm, or sarcasm at this point.

I face frontwards and smile when no one comments on my situation, but I know it's not a total win. Things always manage to come back and bite me in the ass later. This would be no exception.

10: Time Out

T hat night, I sleep well, which is a shocker after the long and tiring conversation I'd had with Finlay after the men's first win. Despite my inner turmoil, worrying about what's going to happen when I return home, I keep a smile plastered on my face, albeit shaky. I can't go on like this forever. There are only so many times I can apologize to my roommate before she starts to complain about my phone calls with Finlay. This morning was even worse than usual.

Coach Kyla eyes me up when I enter the gym. "Sleep well?"

"I did."

She nods, but I know I haven't convinced her. My shoddy performance is proof enough that I'm lying.

After the game, I sneak away from the team, and it's easily accomplished with Savari eating up the attention. I fall behind the main celebration. Even in the highest moment of the weekend, she twists around to make a face at me and make me smile. She's not trying to be a bitch—I know that—and she doesn't have to tell me. I can see what fun I'm missing out on.

Finlay still expects me to call him in between every match with the results. Feeling envious of all the fun they're having, I pull my phone from my bag and sneak free from the team to call Finlay. I jog out to the hall and keep walking until there is some semblance of quiet while I dial home. It's frustrating being this loyal and being treated so poorly. Hiding out so no one knows I'm forced to make these steady calls is embarrassing, but I have to do it. Finlay expects nothing less.

The phone doesn't get off a full ring. "It's about time you called," he answers instantly. "Why don't you put him on the phone?"

"What are you talking about, Finlay? I have no idea what you mean."

"You know damn well what I mean. Put Ryan on the phone."

"Stop it. I don't like what you're insinuating."

"I know you're there with him, Clare. I know that's why you didn't call sooner. I can't believe you'd do this to me after all we've been through."

My coach peeks around the corner and shouts down the hall. "Clarisse, it's time to go."

I bite my lip. "I have to go," I whisper. "I love you and I promise you I'd never do that."

When I end the call, I feel even worse than I did before. A heaviness settles in my chest. It's becoming difficult to breathe. I consider turning off my phone but know that will only prompt a maniacal visit from Finlay. I wouldn't be able to handle that.

When I rejoin the team, Coach Kyla gives me her two cents. "He's no good for you, Clarisse. You're on a downward spiral, aiming for the ground and he's the one driving you there." She pauses long enough for me to meet her eyes. "Are you going to continue to let him? This is on you. You're the only one who decides when to leave. Think about that for a while."

I try to ignore it, wondering why she's even bothering with me, but for the first time, it starts to really sink in. I struggle to get through lunch hour and the next game. It doesn't go very well for the men's team, either. With a massive loss under our belt, the entire team is down in the dumps. No matter what my ladies do to cheer the guys up, everyone settles into a funk and stays there.

Welcome to my club.

Right when I start to think I'm blending in just fine, as everyone boards the buses to return home, Coach Kyla pulls me aside. "Clarisse, listen up, because I'm only going to say this once. You really need to get your priorities straight if you want to stay the head of this team. You're sinking, woman. Ever since you met Finlay, you've been a downer for this team. That man is ruining you and it looks like you've already buckled up for the ride."

Even though she's pulled me aside, I know Savari hears every word of it. Her and that new guy who keeps hitting on her. As my phone buzzes in my bag, I turn away, so they can't read my face. I quickly excuse myself to the restroom to pick up Finlay's call before he thinks something is really up. It's the second time I've heard it going off since I talked to him after the game. Coach Kyla knows exactly what I'm doing, but she lets me go without an argument.

"Hello," I answer softly, as I lock the bathroom door and sit on the edge of the toilet seat fully clothed.

"I'm sorry, baby," Finlay says. "I didn't mean it. You aren't mad at me, are you? I couldn't live with myself if I knew you were upset because of me. Please tell me everything's okay—that we're okay."

Even though I know it's a spastic lie, I tell him. "I'm fine." Truth is I'm still burning from the conversation I had with my coach. How dare she call me out like that and publicly ambush me? Without thinking, I tell him about it.

"Coach Kyla decided to have a little talk with me."

His voice turns hard, but this time it's directed at someone else. "What did she have to say?"

"She says you're bad for me, that I should leave you and focus on the team—get my priorities straight."

His voice turns as cold as a dead body floating in a December lake. "I never liked that bitch."

The conversation doesn't turn much warmer after that. I wish I had a pillow to cry into, but instead I suck it up and hope the strain doesn't show in my face. "I know. I just need a breath," I tell him. "We'll talk when I get home."

I don't know what happens while I'm away, but when I return to the team I'm bombarded by squad members. Savari slings her arm over my shoulder and walks with me the rest of the way to the bus. Coach Kyla lets me have it again—this time in front of the three girls surrounding her. They have obviously been talking about me behind my back.

"This relationship is not good for you. Your boyfriend's destroying your soul," Coach Kyla says. "He's snuffed your light. Things have to change, Clarisse. I'm afraid if you keep this up you won't be recovering because it'll be too late. None of us want that for you."

Savari stops her as my tears start to flow and wash the makeup clean off my face.

Coach Kyla's voice settles, but I can tell she's only worked up because she cares about me. "I'm sorry. I feel very invested in your future, Clarisse. You're a good girl, you've been an amazing teammate, and to see you like this is depressing for everyone watching. You deserve more out of life."

Her words continue to slice me like a knife, but she just keeps talking.

"You can't keep doing this to yourself. You look like shit. We know you're not happy and we're all here for you, if you need us, but you have to let us in. If you don't want to talk to me, fine, but you have to talk to someone."

She walks away, leaving my voice tight in my throat. I flash a glance at Savari but quickly look away. Savari doesn't demand my attention, but her words are just as evocative. She tucks a strand of icy blonde hair behind her ear.

"What are you doing, Clare? If you don't want this guy, okay then, but don't let Coach Kyla make decisions for you. She can't control you, just like he can't. Only you, lady. Think about what you want and then go for it. Don't let anyone—not me, not her, and most certainly not Finn— make your decision for you. Only you." She tucks my index finger against my chest and holds it there to make a point.

I take her offering seriously, silently thanking her with teary eyes and a nod. I start crying and don't stop for a long while. The truth is, I know exactly why I'm crying. Guidance and order is exactly what I need right now. I've been clinging to Coach Kyla's strict schedule and rigorous training because it's the only thing I can rely on. It's the only thing that doesn't hurt in a bad way. It is the only time I have to myself where I can push myself to my limits and forget about the rest of my messed up life.

It is in this moment that I wake up. I will never forget this very second. I love Finlay. I love him more than anyone and anything I've ever loved, myself included. But more than life itself? No.

Hell, no!

I'm having a hard time imagining how I will ever find another man in the future who will love me like he does, but maybe I won't, and that's a good thing. I need some time to myself. I need a chance to have alone time where I can rest my head and do what I want or do nothing at all, for that matter. I only need to regain control of my own life again. I want to make the decisions like I once did.

I can do this.

"When I get home, things are going to change," I admit out loud. My voice is strong and determined, not at all like the cowering woman I've become of late.

Savari squeezes my shoulder and smiles. "I'm glad to hear that. Welcome back, lady."

11: Do It

I can do this. It's not too late to start over. It's time to face my fears and obliterate them.

The bus ride back home seems to take forever and a day. We have another fifteen minutes to go before we're back at the school, and I've already been staring at the back of the seat in front of me for the past ten, procrastinating. On the off chance that an old friend from last year will bail me out of this mess, I text her.

In a bind. Wondering if that spare room you offered me last year is still available.

She instantly responds, but I don't have the nerve to check her answer knowing it will be a flat out no. Ten minutes easily pass before I snap out of it and hunker down for the bad news.

Sorry, it's not.

I figured as much, and why would she bother being nice to me now? It's crazy how quickly my relationship with Finlay has ruined all the other relationships in my life. I toss my phone into my bag and squeeze my eyes shut to keep the tears inside, tilting my head toward the roof of the bus. I settle lower into my seat, wishing I could hide from the world but knowing I have a long way to go before that can happen.

Now what am I supposed to do?

Savari kneels on her seat behind me and peers over my headrest, settling her chin on her hands. "If you're looking for a ride, you can catch one with me. My car is at the school."

I wonder how she knows how I've found myself up shit creek without a paddle. Maybe she was peeking. "How did you—"

"It's all in your sigh and the look on your face." She points at the window next to us. "I saw your reflection."

I nod, smirking at my own stupidity, wondering if Savari

realizes that her offer is just the save I need to keep my head above the water. "Thank you. That would be nice."

I reach for my phone and search for a number I wish I never entered into my contacts—Finlay's mother. I show Savari the picture of the devil herself.

"You can do this," she reminds me as the phone starts to ring.

I put the phone to my ear, take a deep breath, and sit upright, preparing for a fight and getting one. Needless to say, the phone call does not go well.

"I think maybe you should be telling him this," his mother snaps.

I had already told her three times that I have no intention of talking to him about this right now and that he's going to need her attention to get through this. "I can't right now. I just can't."

"Funny, when I asked you whether this was serious, you told me it was."

"It was!" I shout into the phone, growing angry and causing everyone on the bus to stare. I turn toward the window and lower my voice. "This is about as serious as it gets. I'm not coming back."

I want to rip her heart out, but Savari squeezes my shoulder and that calms my nerves just enough to end the call. "Just tell him."

I stare at my phone long after the call has ended.

Savari smiles at me. "You're doing the right thing. It's going to be a tough go for the next little while, but you're going to be all right. If you need a place to stay until you get back on your feet, you're always welcome at my place."

It sure beats staying at the motel across the road. "Savari, you're a lifesaver." But it makes me wonder. "Why are you being so nice to me?"

"Honestly?" she asks, like no one ever calls her out on things like this.

"Yes."

She half shrugs her shoulders. "You were there for me when I needed you. Before Finlay came around, you were

my girl. I see you struggling now and I don't think it's fair
I've practically walked through life without ever having to
worry about where I was going to rest my head at night
You shouldn't have to either. No one deserves what you're
going through. No one."

I smile softly, a little envious to be reminded of how
perfect her life is. "You're really offering me a place to stay?
Because I might just take you up on that."

"Was there somewhere else you were planning on
going?"

I turn my head toward the floor, knowing she doesn't
understand how dire my situation is. "I was afraid I'd be
living in the streets soon, if I didn't figure something out."

Savari knows I spent the better part of my teenage years
bouncing from one foster home to the next. I'd milk the
people around me until they stopped caring enough for me
to stick around. Then I'd move on.

She clasps on to my hand and squeezes, knowing that I'm
remembering horrible pictures of my past, although I never
got around to telling her any of the details. "You're staying
with me."

I twist around and glance up at her—my lifeline. "I
promise to pay you back just as soon as I can."

Her hand gesture shows how unconcerned she is about
the money. "Don't worry about it. My parents are paying the
bills anyways. I'd never take your money."

I hand her everything I have in my wallet, which
admittedly isn't much.

She shakes her head and pushes my hand away as the
bus pulls to a stop. "Not necessary. Seriously, it's fine. Put
your money away."

I tuck the bills away and sigh. If she insists, I'm not going
to push her. It's not like I actually have a boatload of cash to
throw around. I'm broke, except for the four-hundred dollar
scholarship payment I'm expecting next Friday.

When my teammates start to exit the bus, I turn my
attention to the parking lot and scan it for a certain car,
while praying I won't find it. Although I didn't tell Finlay I

was returning at this hour, I know he has other ways of tracking me. Mostly, I'm afraid his mother has already spilled the news, in which case he'll make a beeline for the school—for me.

My stomach bottoms out, empty and scared. I search the parking lot a second time to make sure I haven't missed anything, but he's really not here. The heaviness in my chest only grows heavier. Guilt creeps in and eats me alive. Before my mind snaps in two, Savari breaks the silence.

"Are you coming?"

I grab my bag and follow her off the bus. The sky is dark when I look up above me. Clouds are rolling in, setting up for a vicious storm. With the first drop of rain, I slip into Savari's car and slam the door shut. She takes my bag and throws it into the backseat.

My hands fall to my sides and my palms sink into the soft leather seat. Savari wasn't lying when she said she has it made.

"Don't mind the mess," she says.

I look around the car in search of this mess she speaks of. "What mess, exactly?"

"Isn't it obvious? My car is desperate for a bath. My dad was supposed to send someone over to vacuum it the other day, but the guy never showed."

I have to laugh. "You have someone come and clean your car for you?"

She only then realizes how royally spoiled she is. She smiles my way. "You should bring your car over. He can do yours, too."

I settle back into the chair and crack my window open. "About that."

"Oh, no. Don't tell me."

I scrunch my nose when I look at her. "I sold it. Finlay didn't like me driving the hunk of junk through the city. Especially after our accident and all."

"Mmm, hmm. I'm sure that's exactly why."

"It was falling apart," I admit, all the while wondering why I make excuses for the dumb shit. Finlay wanted me all for himself and that meant disconnecting me from others. Taking my car away was his first move. If I had only realized then what he was doing to me, maybe I could have stopped this from happening. I put my window down to cool my sickly warm cheeks.

"It's not your fault, you know." Savari flashes a glance at me and then checks her mirror. "He would have done anything to keep you under his wing. You'll see someday soon that you're being used. He wants you to believe you're his crutch, but he's a master manipulator. You could stand to learn a lesson or two from him."

I get it—control—it's all about control. It's time for me to regain some of that for myself. It's crazy how with the wind breezing through my hair and rain sprinkling on my cheeks, I feel so free. Even though I now hold the key to my own fate, that feeling won't last long, as I've learned time and time again in my life. I'm not allowed to be happy. That's just the life dealt to me, and it is time I am reminded of that eternal debt, the hard way—always the hard way.

12: D-Day

I don't have any clean clothes, and I can't imagine going to school on Monday wearing Savari's designer digs. It's bad enough I'm mooching off her for food and a roof over my head. People will already be talking. The last thing I need is people thinking I left Finlay for my wealthy lesbian lover, although it might be easier to explain things to Finlay that way.

After a long conversation with Savari, we agree it's probably best to get this out of the way tonight, rather than dragging it out for everyone to witness at school tomorrow. It's half past eleven when we reach my house—*his* house. My stomach feels twisted like a pretzel when I get out of Savari's car with the empty duffle bag. I knew this was going to be hard, but damn, my stomach is cramping, and I'm having second thoughts. I walk up Finlay's short driveway to the front door of the house.

Do I knock?

A lick of lightning startles me. Savari hops out of the driver's seat and stands at her open door when she sees how I've frozen at the base of the front steps. "Want me to come with?"

I tilt my head toward her and smile. She's backlit from a street lamp while I'm surrounded in darkness. "I really don't think you want to do that. This is messy enough as it is."

"Moral support," she offers, teasing me slightly.

I'm happy she's trying to lighten the mood, but the situation is rather serious, and I don't want to drag her into my problems any further. "No, it's okay. If you don't mind, I'll just run in there real quick and get my things. I shouldn't be long at all."

"Okay. I'll be here," she answers with a gentle smile. "Don't let him push you around."

"I won't."

"Good luck?" she adds hesitantly.

Yeah, luck.

When I stand there a second too long, Savari helps me on my way. "Get out of here!"

"I'm going," I insist, but I struggle to take the first step up the porch.

I'm stronger than the girl I was yesterday.

I turn back to Savari, second guessing my strength. She lifts up both of her thumbs, wearing an exaggerated smile.

I have to do this.

I lift a fisted hand to knock on the door. I need my things for tomorrow. I told Finlay's mother I was coming over, and she didn't say no. A quick in and out. That's all it'll be.

Knock. Knock. Knock.

The door creaks open, and I find his glaring mother on the other side of the open door. Was she listening to me this entire time? She opens the door wide and steps aside without saying much. I kick off my shoes and wait for her to say something more.

"He's in his room." She turns to walk away but quickly turns back to me. "If you're leaving him, make it a nice clean break, will you? You owe him that much."

I don't respond to her, because nothing I think to say is very nice. When it appears to be safe to walk away, she turns back again. "Remember, you did this to him."

I scowl in her direction, saving my strength for Finlay. She takes the hint and goes to hide out in her bedroom, the door closing firmly behind her. With a steadying breath, I walk across the house lit only by the lamp in the front room and the light from the moon. I head right for Finlay's closed bedroom door and stop just outside of it.

What am I doing here? I shouldn't have come alone. This is a bad idea.

Standing very still, I convince myself that we can sort this out like grown adults. I'll tell him I'm leaving, stuff a couple days' worth of clothes into my duffle bag, and take off. And like that, I'll be a free woman. *Easy peasy.*

With renewed determination, I knock on the bedroom

door. That's when all hell breaks loose.

"Come in," Finlay shouts. His voice is edgy and angry. I can tell he's been crying.

I get it. He's upset. I hate that I'm doing this to him but know it's the only way for me to survive. I swallow the lump in my throat and take another deep breath that doesn't quite reach my lungs. My heart is racing at an unbearable rate. When I step inside his room, the empty bag I've been carrying drops from my trembling fingers.

"Whoa, stop!" I scream, hoping the whole neighborhood will hear and come to my rescue.

"We have to die, Clarisse. It's the only way for us to be together."

"No!" All the color flushes out of my face as hot tears rush down my cheeks.

He nods, affirming his plan. "It's the only way."

I know I should turn around and run through the open door, but my feet are glued to the old beige carpet, and I remain standing there like a deer in headlights. He lifts the handgun with a straight arm and points it directly at my face.

I don't move, too scared for what might happen if I do. "No," I cry, but it doesn't matter. He's already made up his mind. I close my eyes for only a second, not liking the feeling of the cold revolver pressing against my forehead.

"I'm going to do it," he warns me, cocking the gun with a sickening click.

His grip falters. My eyes flit open as he readjusts his finger. I'd already believed him before. Now that I see the rope dangling loosely from the ceiling and the small stool propped beneath it, I know I'm screwed.

"In case I chicken out after you go," he explains, like it's a logical explanation.

I notice something else out of place and draw my eyes to the dresser where I once stored my undergarments. The street light glares off a collection of large knives decorating the top of it, laid out in order from smallest to largest.

"Your heart is and will always be mine," he explains. "I

was going to let you pick which way you wanted to go, but now I think I'll decide."

My knees give out when I realize what he means. Those knives are meant for me. I crash onto the floor, and it takes me a second to recover. Breathing heavily, I find myself sitting on the dingy carpet that I now see is littered with my things. First, I locate my one and only pair of expensive shoes. I cringe when I realize the dislocated high-heel is buried beneath the clothes I'd purchased with the last of my parents' credit, every garment ripped into two pieces.

I try to hold in my revulsion, but there are handcuffs dangling from the leather computer chair. The room looks like a sick horror show. Pick your poison.

"I don't understand," I say with a hushed voice, filled with emotion. I get on all fours and try to pull myself up to my feet but fail when Finlay punctures my neck with a syringe, knocking me back to the floor.

I grab at my neck. "What the fuck?"

"Don't move," is Finlay's response. He pushes the door shut and, within seconds, my arms feel numb. He leans in close and I wince, afraid he's ready to begin with the torture.

"Please, Finlay. No," I cry, smelling a rank odor emanating from his inebriated skin.

How had I not seen this coming?

I catch the flash of the alarm clock when it strikes eleven eleven but just barely through the wet tears. I make a wish, knowing how stupid that is at a time like this. Minutes pass like hours. Had he known I would come to him? I slowly settle back onto my calves. I have to do something. My life cannot end like this, but everything is getting blurry.

"I love you, baby," he says, right before I feel the cold circular barrel press back into my upturned forehead. I don't make it easy for him, staring straight into his eyes.

Still, his finger squeezes the tiny metal flange until the gun clicks. My stomach instantly lurches, and I bend forward to gag, but nothing comes out. Finlay has decided he is going to take my life. He pulled the trigger. I should have died. But reality has a humorous side. The gun must have jammed. Either that or Finlay hasn't loaded it properly. Regardless, a bullet hasn't fired, and my face is still wholly intact.

Finlay's confused now but not half as confused as I am. He looks down the barrel of the gun, slapping the thing, crying into the hole.

"Why?"

He points it at me again, this time at my chest, confirming my greatest fear. "You were supposed to die."

I barely manage to stumble to my feet, holding both my hands forward in a hesitant surrender. Finlay tries to push the revolver toward me, but this time I fight back. I will not feel that thing touching my skin again. With a screech, I karate chop his arm in a violent attempt to save my face. A single shot discharges from the barrel and another quickly follows. Finlay crashes into me with the force of gravity, taking us both to our knees.

A warm, thick liquid rolls down my face, reminding me that I am all flesh and bones. A dark crimson color has splattered the wall and drips from my eyes like a leaky faucet. Like a flame being snuffed, the revolting sight steals all the oxygen from my lungs and sucks me dry of awareness. I hold my breath, my stomach wavering, with the weight of death tugging me toward the floor. I wait for death to take me, staring into Finlay's heavy shoulder.

Will I be so lucky?

13: The Rising Sun

I've fallen to my knees, staring into Finlay's shoulder, waiting for him to finish me—or maybe he already has. The dark red blood trickling down my face is warm and pasty, and my body grows heavier in a moment of silence. It takes a second for me to realize that it's Finlay's body that has gone limp. When I push his dead weight off of me, he falls to the floor with a thump that would haunt a good part of me for the rest of my days.

With a few blinks, I realize I am mostly unharmed, except for the slurred speech, tingling fingers, and punctured skin. I instantly grab at my neck and then run my fingers over my face, searching for the source of the blood but only smearing it around. The blood on my face is not mine. The brain splatter on the wall is that of Finlay—my love. I slowly swipe a bit from my cheek, too stunned by this turn of events to respond with emotion.

Finlay drips from the walls and a dark crimson color oozes all over the floor. I stare at the pile of man for what feels like a long time, although in reality only a moment passes. I look for a distinguishable feature on Finlay's face—anything to identify him as my living, breathing Finlay—but I don't find one.

He's dead. Finlay's dead.

"Help," I whisper but my voice is barely audible. I feel gutted, like my insides have been stripped of all major organs. But how do you react when it's your own doing? I've no one to scream at but myself.

I begin to cry, selfishly. "You can't die. You just can't. Please!" I scream hysterically. "No!" I grab on to his shirt and try to shake his rumpled form, but he's too heavy.

He's already dead.

My voice comes back to me with a vengeance. My scream seems to echo indefinitely. I don't remember stopping, except to vomit. Mrs. Turnbull bursts into the room first, followed by my best friend, Savari. I don't meet either of their eyes, dizziness taking me. I know what they're thinking. Horrific voices screech and cry out for help until the sirens arrive.

Now, I'm not in any sort of shape to think clearly, and there is much that I can't remember from that night, but in life there are some lessons you never forget. It was on that night I learned it only takes one shot at close range for a man to blow his own face clean off, and that's exactly what I said to the authorities.

14: Downward Spiral

If I'd been asked to say a few words at Finlay's funeral, which I hadn't, I would have compared him to cancer. He'd latched on to my body—clutched on tightly—and dragged me toward a cruel demise, but not before suffocating the life right out of me. He left me no other option but to fall to my knees and beg for my life back, because that's what he'd taken from me, and so that's what I did.

That day at the church, after sitting through the depressing revelations from friends and family I've never even met and struggling with the ill-informed stares from people who blamed me for Finlay's accident, I snap. While praying to the high heavens and begging for forgiveness, something happens—*and not something good*.

All my sad thoughts, silence, and grief morph into disturbing feelings that have always been there, festering just below the surface. That nasty frame of mind bubbles up now, intensified by Finlay's ultimate selfish act. That greed rides me like a wave, an indulgence I grant myself while I gamble away my sanity in exchange for freedom.

Finlay has ruined me. I offered him my virginity, and he stole my innocence, my spirit, and my light. Life with him was torture, but life without him is something else entirely. *What ifs* plague me, pushing me to the edge, leading me down a path that'll take me nowhere good. I hop onto a downward spiral, all those nasty stares eroding my care for all humanity.

Something is different now. Suddenly, I'm not the innocent one anymore. I see the way people stare. It's not so much fear I see, as it is curiosity. Did she kill him? Will she do it again? But no one has the nerve to ask me. Not my teachers. Not my friends. Not Finlay's family. In fact, the only person with the gall to ask is the police detective who looks like he has a chip on his shoulder.

He doesn't even see through my lies. None of them understand how I feel inside. I'm done being a doormat. I told him what happened. Finlay flailed a gun around in a torture chamber meant for me. He tried to kill me. His plan backfired. When he tried to see what went wrong with the gun, it blasted his face off. No one was present in that room except for me and him. We are the only ones who will ever know the truth, and since Finlay's dead now, I can say whatever the hell I want, and they have no choice but to believe it.

I turn up the tears and take a week off of school, but my mind plays nasty tricks on me. Dare I say I'm happy by this turn of events? Savari has given me a place to stay, much nicer than the place I was staying at before, and Finlay's mother is convinced to replace all of my belongings that were ruined by Finlay's outburst and now splattered with his blood and brain matter. She didn't have much of a choice. It was either that or she makes an insurance claim, but her lawyers told her she didn't want to do that with the evidence stacked against her son.

I hold up my designer heels and smile. *Thank you, Mrs. Turnbull.*

A few weeks have passed since Finlay was buried, and I find that I have a lot of spare time on my hands. All this free time opens up a new venue for finding temporary relief. I go out at night and make new friends of the male variety. Savari seems to think that I'm drinking to wash away the horrible feelings brought on by Finlay's death, and that I'm letting men touch me because I'm lonely, but the truth is I enjoy the attention and the control.

Every weekend, I try on a different flavor of man: tall, short, firm, fat, hard, and soft. In public, I tease them to the point of erupting. When they ask me to leave with them, I say yes. Everyone around me believes these men are getting lucky. Every single time, I've escaped to *use the restroom* and then disappeared out the back. It's a dangerous game I'm playing, but I keep at it until I've secretly seduced a good portion of the men's basketball team.

No one says a thing about it to me. The guys take off and let everyone believe I left with them. They probably rush home to whack off. I don't know why they keep their lips sealed. I figure they're either ashamed for taking advantage of the lonely widowed girlfriend, or they're unwilling to tarnish their chances of getting laid by me in the future.

In reality, taking another man to my bed is the last thing I need right now. I was made to suffer by a man, and now man will suffer from my wrath. With all this time spent drinking and dreaming up my revenge, I'm barely scraping by at school. It's amazing how quickly your GPA can take a nosedive after you've seen the inside of your boyfriend's head.

It looks like I'm going to have to put my new prowess to work while trying out my new shoes. Something has to give or I'm not going to get through this school year. I'm not about to repeat it because of this one man. I'll have to do something drastic to fix this.

Knock. Knock. Knock.

I adjust my black dress so my tits look extra perky, the flesh of my cleavage visible to anyone who's looking. Mr. Varela shouts for me to go away but I'm persistent.

Knock. Knock. Knock.

Convincing my first three teachers to fix my grade was a cinch. Even the short lesbian lady was open to my less than traditional tactics. I was shocked to learn they only needed tears, when I was fully prepared to make it worth their while. Mr. Varela, I'm afraid, will need a little more convincing. I've saved him for last. I'm not below begging.

Mr. Varela is the youngest of them all, handsome, married, head of the Psychology department, and a stickler for the rules. I don't even need his sympathy at this point; my GPA will probably be fine now that my other teachers have heard my sob story. But there's something stopping me from turning down the challenge. Varela's alpha composure attracts me, for one. The fact that he's married makes me want to try my luck even more. I need to know whether all men are that selfish, or if it was just Finlay.

Knock. Knock. Knock. Knock.

I glance down the hallway. It's late. Most of the students and many of the teachers have long ago left for the night. He's one of those professors—you know the type—who stays late every night to keep on top of things. I've heard he's not the type who mingles with students. By your third year, you get a good grasp of which profs are faithful and which ones are dirty dogs. Everyone has placed Mr. Varela strictly among those in that first category. I tend to agree with them, but I'm not afraid to gamble.

I've been working on him for days, and I believe I've found a glitch I plan to capitalize on tonight. He's often cold and arrogant, but he's attracted to innocence and awkward apologies. I can be whoever he wants me to be. I look forward to it. No matter the cost.

Knock. Knock. Knock. Knock. Knock.

"All right, all right," he growls, his anger and exasperation laughable.

He throws the door open, his eyes landing on my chest and his mouth falling slack before he can check himself. He quickly recovers but I've already seen what I needed to see. As I suspected, underneath that perfectly laundered suit and good manners is a man with raw needs and a desire to satisfy them.

"Good evening, Mr. Varela."

His expression softens when he finds my face on top of my boobs. I know this is my chance, as he takes a step back into his office. He nods at me. "Miss Blackwell."

I love how he already senses his own weakness. He hasn't shut me out. There's another win in my future yet.

I mimic his frustration. "I'm sorry. It's late. You're busy. I shouldn't have come."

His response comes quickly. "No, no. It's quite all right. Please."

He offers for me to take a seat in front of his desk. When I enter his office, the temperature in the room spikes a few degrees, and I flourish in the knowledge that he's reacting to my presence. Before I sit down, I turn to face him.

"What can I do you for—do for you! What can I do for you?" he corrects rather loudly.

My teeth sink into my lower lip as I feign embarrassment.

"Sorry, long day," he admits, and I would have believed him if his eyes hadn't settled on my porcelain skin and then lit up when he noticed the warmth reaching my cheeks.

If he thought his day was long, it's about to get a whole lot longer. I twist away and move toward the door, but he rushes over to stop me.

"I can come back another time," I explain, turning my eyes to the floor.

His hand slides onto my shoulder and squeezes, like he's supporting a student torn from youth by her tragic life experience. I can't help but smile, barely managing to keep it hidden from him.

"I'd like to help you."

I peer up at him wearing that wickedly aroused smile. "But you already have."

He swallows, snaps out of it, and closes his door. He's new at this—nervous—but he knows full well what he's doing. He doesn't lock his door or usher me out of it. He does lose the masculine grace that I've come to love from a distance as he walks toward his desk. The way he trips over himself is kind of cute.

"Please, sit."

I take a seat this time, without hesitation. "I hate to trouble you."

"No, no trouble," he says, perching on the corner of his desk.

I love the way his buttoned-up shirt strains across his chest when he folds his arms across it. The thoughtful expression on his face is convincing. His jaw is strong but tense. His body is rigid and confident, but his eye twitches from behind those intelligent glasses when I cross my legs. The fact that he notices the way my dress inches higher up my thighs tells me he's struggling to maintain that steely composure.

I take advantage of that small victory and smile. "You don't have to be ashamed for looking, Mr. Varela. I actually enjoy having your eyes on me almost as much as I'm going to enjoy your lips."

He shakes his head like he's misheard me. "Huh? What?" I let him believe that he has for the moment.

"I was hoping you could give me a hand with something."

"Of course. Anything. What is it?"

He doesn't wait for me to pull work out of my bag. He knows exactly what kind of help I'm referring to. I've grown tired of spending my nights seducing the dumb jocks and easy targets. I want to know what it's like to bring a successful, intelligent man down. I want to be the subject of all his desires so that I can hold his life in my hands and rip it out from underneath him. It'll be nice for someone else to understand what it feels like to be at rock bottom—like I do.

"There's this thing that's been plaguing me and I think you're the answer I've been looking for." I uncross my legs and spread them apart, with my hands pushing the insides of my knees until they're wide enough apart for him to see something that students should keep covered in their professor's office, even if I did shave especially for him. He stares, shamelessly, it finally dawning on him that I'm not wearing any panties.

"I, uh. No. I, I, I mean," he stutters, retracting his refusal. He lifts his glasses, covers his eyes with one hand, and lets out a heavy sigh of pent up sexual frustration. "I can't."

I push to my feet, but my dress stays hiked up like a good mini skirt should, just barely hiding my goodies. "You can't? Or you won't?" I slide my hands up and down his solid chest, waiting for him to break. I chew on my bottom lip again, drawing his eyes to the ruby color before dropping to my knees. I have his belt undone before he even realizes what I plan to do. His eyes zero in on my puckered red lips as I stroke him through his pants.

He shakes his head, but he doesn't pull my hands away, and I'm close to having his zipper down. "I can't," he chants repeatedly as I tug down his pants and pull him out of his briefs.

Holy, shit. We have a winner! Mr. Varela is packing, and whatever I'm doing must be working because he's as hard as it gets, and I haven't even put him in my mouth yet. I tease him first, allowing my red lips to wrap around all that man and slide down the length of him. He is astonished, overwhelmed, and speechless. So am I! Almost.

"What's wrong, Mr. Varela? Cat got your tongue?"

He gives up the fight and weaves his fingers into my hair, guiding the depth and speed of penetration to his liking. He's close. It hasn't been but seconds, and he's already close. When I know he's past the point of no return, I pull away, breaking the seal.

"Wait," he pleads, stroking himself, maintaining his hardness.

I can't believe how erotic and appealing I find him right now. This was not a part of the plan. "Yes?"

"I need more. Please," he begs.

I push him backwards until he's lying on his back, his man parts standing perpendicular to his desk. I hike my dress over my hips and crawl over him, propping myself over a very erect cock.

"Wait," he pleads, warring with himself.

Without battling it out, I lower myself onto him, just slightly. He's barely past my entrance, throbbing where we touch, when he groans. Oh, yes, I'm wet, too. He sighs again, as I let him dip in a little farther before he makes his final decision.

"I can't fuck you," he moans, even though he's already inside me.

It's a little late for that, I would say. "Then sit still and enjoy the ride." I lower myself onto him, my tightness encircling him slowly, until he's completely buried in my warmth.

He closes his eyes and groans, appreciating the tightness, his fingers involuntarily digging into my hips.

I rock forward, taking him as deeply as I want. I expect him to sit back and be still, but he can't do it. Instead, he leans forward and takes my mouth against his, his tongue seeking out mine, kissing me with that very expert tongue. He grabs on to my ass with two rough hands, working himself deeper and deeper, until he's the one thrusting upwards into me.

I lean back with my mouth partially agape and his lips naturally magnetize to the soft flesh of my neck. Shit. I didn't want to enjoy this. This wasn't supposed to be this much fun. But as Mr. Varela rams into me, I find myself swirling with desire and shocked by the way my orgasm suddenly takes me. He stiffens seconds later, holding me sensually, like a lover, his lips pressed into my throat.

Neither of us speaks, but I can't stop smiling. Now that was fun! He twists off the side of his desk and helps me off of his semi-hard dick. I put my feet on the floor one at a time, my heels clicking with each step. I cross the room, where I find and retrieve my purse.

"Thank you, Mr. Varela. You've been most helpful."

After pulling his pants up to his waist, he lifts his glasses and covers his eyes with a masculine hand. "Zayne," he says. He peers at me from under that guilty salute. "Call me Zayne."

We exchange glances as I pull on some underwear. He does up his pants and readjusts his tie, throwing it aside when he realizes that righting himself is a lost cause. He might regret this in an hour from now, but I guarantee you, he'll be coming back for more. They always do.

15: Blackmail

Blackmail is such a dirty word but not half as dirty as the deed my prof has succumbed to: a married man screwing a cheerleader who happens to also be his student. You're probably wondering whether we've done it again. We most certainly have, each time getting more exhilarating and risqué than the last. Somebody might have even snapped a few web shots of me pressed into the wall, half naked with Zayne's pants around his ankles—you know, for my screensaver, or maybe his wife's.

Mr. Zayne Varela has no idea what he's gotten himself into. He's too high on young pussy to realize I am the poison that's going to ruin his career and marriage. All this power goes straight to my head and fuels my yearning for more. There are some days I wish I could just roll over and die. Other days—like today—I feel a strength I never knew existed.

I wasn't planning on making an appearance at my graduation ceremony knowing the event is going to be a bore, and it is, beyond dreadful, but to see Zayne's face when I shake his hand and exchange a photograph for my diploma will be worth all the glowering at the cute couple holding hands next to me. I'm up next, so I climb the stairs and wait for the announcer to call my name.

"Clarisse Blackwell."

Mr. Varela startles, searching the throng of graduates for me. There's a commotion in the audience and a gang of cheerleaders and basketball players hoot from the back of the room.

"Ow ow!" is the last thing I hear before the president of the school shakes my hand.

"Good luck in your future endeavours," she tells me.

"Thank you." I don't need anyone's well wishes and words of wisdom, and I most certainly don't need her pity. But there it is, in her eyes. Yeah, I'm that girl. At least I *was*.

Get over it.

Standing next to the president of the school is Mr. Varela, looking as handsome as ever in his sophisticated grey suit. He extends his right hand for a firm shake, just the same as he has for every other graduate, handing me my diploma with his other hand.

"Zayne," I say, wearing a coy smile as a journalism student snaps our photograph, our eyes intimately connected in that moment.

When I reach for my diploma, our hands touch and there's electricity there. I squeeze his other hand firmly when his fingers brush over mine. If he's comfortable being that daring, then I can be, too. I breathe something in his ear, slipping a folded paper into his pocket. Anyone in the crowd might think I am slipping him my phone number, and that's exactly what I want it to look like.

The graduates ahead of me exit the stage, but I hold on to his gaze as I walk away from him. Does he not realize that this kind of eye contact is inappropriate? I want him to remember what we've done, what I'm going to do to him next.

He knows.

Instead of following the other graduates back to my seat, after flipping the tassel on my hat, I walk straight out the back door of the gymnasium, meeting up with my friends in the hall.

"Clarisse!" Savari shouts when she sees me walking toward them. She leans in to privately whisper the rest. "What the hell was that all about?"

I shrug my shoulders, hoping everyone else noticed the way Mr. Varela regarded me.

We arrive at a local bar, and the rumors have already sprung up from the woodworks. One hour passes. Then two. I watch the door obsessively, but Zayne doesn't appear. For the next three hours, I become drunk on my hatred for men—for life. I'm drunk because I'm miserable. Miserable, because I'm lonely and my plan has backfired. And I'm mad, because no matter how many men I successfully pursue—

no matter how much fire Zayne brings to the desk—nothing fills the void of unconditional love.

Nothing.

As the night progresses, rumors fly and grow into a web of suspicion and lies. People start calling me the Black Widow, to my face and behind my back. They say now I'm going after the wealthy professional, because I didn't make anything off of my poor-ass student boyfriend. Are they right? I don't even know anymore.

I stumble to the bar and order another shot, overhearing the guy next to me talking about a woman who killed the man she loved, with a gun to his head. When he realizes I'm that woman, he covers his mouth with a hand—like, oh shit—and stops talking. I can't even deny it. It's true.

I killed my first love. He's dead, much like my soul.

I drop a ten dollar bill on the bar, down my shot, and walk away. Making eye contact with Savari from across the room, I point to where I'm heading. She doesn't follow, though, looking pretty busy with her other people. I slump onto an empty stool and rest my head against a sticky table.

People aren't being fair. Some things are my fault, but the things I'm being accused of just aren't true. You want the truth? Ask the cops. I told them the truth at first. They said it was the drugs talking. Finlay had drugged me, and I told the detective exactly what happened. I told him it was all my fault. I told him Finlay would be alive if it weren't for me.

He didn't believe me.

Secretly, I believe he thinks Finlay deserved it, and since it was Finlay who had his finger on the trigger, he's the responsible party. The police had taken me in, mostly because Finlay's mother is a selfish bitch, but they quickly cleared my name, and Savari's lawyer had me home by the time the sun rose the next day.

The lawyers tell me I'm *not guilty*. The cop told me I only said what I said because of the mental state I was in. They were right about one thing: I wasn't in my right mind. I said what the lawyers told me to say, like a robot. I cried when they told me to cry, jumping through the hoops like a good old dog. They say I'm *not guilty*. It doesn't mean it's true.

The entire scenario continues on replay in my mind. I can't help but feel like the whole incident is a cruel, cruel joke being played on me.

This life is a fucking joke. Oh, but the trick is on me!

Zayne's not here. I gave him one shred of control, and here I am, waiting for him like the loser mistress. Life is not fair. I don't want to be here anymore, but the last shred of goodness left in this shell of a body won't allow me to take my own life. There are many nights when I struggle with the idea—like tonight. Maybe I am the Black Widow. Maybe I deserve to die, too.

First, my parents died and then my first love. *Who's next?*

Unfortunately for me that answer would come soon enough.

16: Ruby Red

I slick on another coat of ruby red lip stick and smack my lips together. Looking this good after what I've been through should be a crime. Savari hooks on to my elbow and drags me out of the restroom. "Come on. Everyone's waiting for us "

I let her pull me through the crowd to a group of cheerleaders hanging off the basketball team. I don't know what she's talking about. No one's waiting for me. They're all celebrating the finish of another school year, so I try to act like I'm okay with being here. I swallow the shots and fake a smile, but I'm dead inside.

Everyone else seems to be living it up—everyone but one guy sitting alone at a table with a ball cap pulled low, nursing a beer. Even though I can't see his face, he manages to snake my attention every minute or so. No one talks to him, and he makes no effort to get involved in any of the nonsensical conversations.

The basketball captain snags my attention with a concerned look on his face. Ryan's supposed to be celebrating his graduation tonight, but he's not wearing a smile like everyone else in the place. He glances around awkwardly, watching people. For a second, I actually think we might have something in common.

"Hey," he says.

"Hey, Ryan."

His night must be going shitty like mine, by the way he looks at me, but I read him all wrong. As he leans into me, I push his shoulder away, and he raises both hands in surrender. "I just wanted to tell you something, and I figured you might not want everyone to hear."

My insides twist into a knot and slosh among the liquor in my stomach.

"There's someone here to see you."

My eyes flash to the door, but Zayne isn't there. My eyes

flicker from one huddle of drunks to the next. Shit, why are my hopes up? I look to Ryan, and he points at the dude sitting alone a few tables over. With confusion marking my face, I walk toward the guy. The dude squints at me from under the peak of his hat. I remain fixated on him and the assault of his sudden smile floods my body with endorphins.

There's something to be said for a man with such an honest smile. He makes me curious and intrigued, when all I've felt for the past few hours is sorrow and regret. Just as I reach the table, one of the girls from my squad swoops in and attacks him with a hug.

"Mr. Varela! I thought that was you!"

He shrugs her off, like the slut she is and makes certain I notice the way he blatantly ignores her. Ryan grabs the girl's arm and walks away with her, stealing all the attention away from Zayne and me. I remain silent, without an expression on my face, because I don't want to admit that I'm happy to see him. I cling to the back of the empty bar stool next to him, unwilling to accept the fact that his constant reassurance makes me want more for myself.

I focus on the fact that he's an asshole—the one who's been sitting here all along and did not once make a move to acknowledge me. He could have saved me from myself tonight, but he didn't, like he isn't now. He continues to nurse his beer, hovering over it with his hat blocking his eyes, as if he hasn't noticed that I haven't so much as brushed the arm of another man this evening.

I get it. He's not here for me. I doubt any man with half a brain would even want to be seen with a woman heading backwards in life, especially such a gifted professor as Zayne Varela. I tear my eyes away from him and turn toward the dance floor, just now noticing the music has turned slow. A sleazy R & B song has all the couples grinding and, when I spin back to my friends, I realize they've all partnered off already. *Wonderful.*

The only person hanging around who I recognize is a short dude from my class who's been desperately pursuing me since freshman year. He moves closer and smiles up into my eyes. In this moment, I feel nothing but utter disappointment. His itchy, brown suit jacket rubs against my arm, and I step backwards, hoping I don't get a rash from it.

"Will you dance with me, Clarisse?" he begs.

Is this what my life has come to? Will I be forced to accept an overweight and short statured man who I'm not even attracted to, so I don't have to be alone?

Itchy suddenly scurries away, but not before I notice the size of his eyes growing like big, black saucers. I wait a second, and then whirl around to see why he's taken off in such a hurry. Zayne is standing behind me, so close my hair lands partly on his shoulder when I spin around. I quickly retrieve my hair, wrap it around my hand, and pull it over my shoulder, frowning softly with down-turned eyes.

What am I supposed to say to him when he's standing there silently staring at the fullness of my mouth? Feeling defeated, I ask him, "What are we doing here?"

"You know exactly what we're doing here. Are you scared?"

Something about him makes me feel like a dangerous woman. I laugh morbidly. "No."

"Good," he says, but he makes no motion to move any closer to me. Is he afraid someone will see us together in public? It feels like he wants to move in to kiss me, but his feet remain planted firmly in place, and his chin doesn't waiver.

"If you're expecting something from me, you're going to have to lay it out there," I say. "I've had too much to drink for you to pussyfoot around anything and expect me to know what the hell I'm supposed to do here."

"You just keep being you."

I swoon for the first time in a long time, feeling a little stunned beneath the dimpled cheeks of this man and, even though I allow myself that one small pleasure, it's obvious he's still tiptoeing around something. "If you're waiting for the perfect time to make our relationship public, be honest with yourself, that's never."

Zayne presses a finger over my pursed lips to hush them and then drops his hand to his side. "I'm not here to argue, and I'm not about to waste words trying to fix what can't be unbroken."

The memory of Finlay's crumpled body haunts me. Is Zayne referring to my sensibilities? I try harder to understand what he means. Why are his eyes so soft? I swear they're filled with compassion.

"Stop right there," I say.

He lifts his hands and backs away. "I wasn't doing anything."

"You most certainly were. I see it in your doughboy eyes. You feel bad for me. Quit feeling bad for me."

"I don't feel bad for you."

I mimic his stance and cover my breasts with folded arms. "You do. You must have been watching me. You know I'm stuck in my own living hell and you don't want to be a part of it. Just say it."

"Wrong," he admits. "If I feel bad for anything, it's for feeling the way I do about you." He lowers his voice and moves in closer to me. "It's for not telling you the truth about my situation and for dragging you along for the ride."

Huh? I'm sure my face says it all. What the hell is he talking about *his situation*?

His face softens a little more, and he holds a hand out to the dance floor with the other one slipping to the small of my back. "There will be plenty of time for that later. For now, I say we dance."

I shake my head, disagreeing with him while my body is awakened by the tender way he touches the bare skin just above my skin-tight jeans. Dancing is the last thing I want to do right now, and sex is the last thing I need on my mind, but I love the feel of his hands on me and can't ignore the promise in his voice when he begs me to join him on the dance floor.

"Please?" he whispers darkly.

It makes my breath hitch and my heartbeat accelerate. I

feel my feet moving, while my head is somewhere else.

Without waiting for an actual response, he leads me across the room. It feels like I'm floating behind him. He doesn't pay attention to all the people around us but stares back into my eyes, wearing that dimpled smile. What now? Why did he stop?

"You're going to have to put your arms around me if we're going to do this." He smirks at me and slings my arms over his shoulders, drawing me close. When he loops his arms around my waist, I feel him mold our bodies together. Nothing has ever felt more perfect.

I can't even speak, so I don't bother trying. I just inhale the amazing scent coming from his T-shirt and tilt my head to rest it against his shoulder. One of his arms curls up my back and presses me into him completely. I close my eyes, comforted by that glorious scent and the deep rumble of his voice humming the song. The vibrations soothe me with relief I haven't felt in years.

Ignoring the way everyone watches us, I fall into the pools of wonder in his eyes and bask there with trembling lips. I refuse to allow any insecurity to shine through when I ask for what I want. My voice comes out sounding sultry. "Kiss me."

He smiles and heat sweeps through my lips, making them tingle. I *need* him to kiss me, and that one and only thought consumes me while we continue to dance, and I continue to gaze up into his eyes. His body remains very erect, but his lips don't drop toward mine. His smile fades off. What a surprise, he's uncertain whether he's made the right decision in coming here tonight. More negative thoughts swoop in while I outwardly war with a devilish smile, waiting for his response.

He adjusts his hat to cover his eyes and then pulls one of my hands out from behind his neck and kisses my knuckles. It's clear now that he has no intention of kissing me. He lowers my hand and pulls me closer. I crash back into his chest, feeling like a complete tool. He holds me there, without another word. How have I allowed myself to miss the fact that I'm not the one in control here anymore?

The school year is over. Our relationship is over. He doesn't need me anymore. This is obviously his way of breaking it to me easily. *How stupid am I?*

Tears spring to my eyes and I let them fall. I don't even care at this point. Zayne doesn't even realize I'm drenching his shirt until I hiccup. His hands instantly come up to cup my face, as he forces me to meet his eyes.

"Hey, what's going on?"

The waterworks just hit me, and I literally cannot turn them off. I snuff, with tears continuing to fall. "I don't know," I whisper, even though I totally do. I am ruined for him. I brought this beautiful man here, and he left a woman just like me at home. I did that. What have I become?

His right hand slides through my hair and clutches me gently against his chest. "I don't want to tarnish this moment."

"Then kiss me," I beg him, as if that will make the tears go away.

Zayne shakes his head. "Not here. Not tonight."

I feel embarrassed. "When, then?" He knows I'm not talking about the kiss anymore, and I know the answer is never. I was dumb to believe this affair could become anything more than a little extracurricular fun.

We stop dancing, and he gives me a sideways glance. "Come on. This is not the place for this."

For what—crying? I was getting good at that lately. In public, though? This is a new low for me. I know it will taint my bad-girl reputation if anyone else notices, so I hide the emotions and let him pull me across the room. He tells Savari he's taking me home. She waves at me, with a curiosity that I know I'll have to answer to tomorrow.

No further words are exchanged as he draws me outside and tucks me into his fancy SUV. I watch him get in and start the gas guzzler, but again he doesn't speak of any of it. The faint music swallows me whole. He gives me nothing, not even an awkward glance.

Fifteen minutes later, I'm shocked to find that I'm

standing next to him at the curb in front of Savari's house He certainly hasn't wasted any time getting rid of me. Zayne takes my hand and leads me to the front porch. He stops at the painted wooden stairs, leaving me to climb them myself. I take two steps up and turn around once I realize he's not following me.

"So this is how it ends?"

He shakes his head. "That's not it at all."

"Right." Am I really supposed to believe this bullshit?

"There are a few things you need to know about me." He sighs.

Here we go. "Is this the, *I'm sorry but I'm married* routine? It's fine. Save it for next year's pick."

"Clarisse," he growls. "Will you stop for one second?"

I lift my eyes and stare him down, waiting for him to speak.

"I'm not married. There, I said it."

"What?" I can't believe my ears. That's the last thing I expected to come out of his mouth.

"We've been separated for about a year and a half now, but we were living under the same roof. You don't know this, because I don't share my personal life with my students and no one needs to know how Casey has taken me for everything I m worth. The last thing I need are rumors milling about." He swipes a tired hand over his face.

I almost start to feel sorry for him. "And you've decided to tell me this now, of all nights, because..."

"I'm afraid you think this is a fun little trick you're pulling on me. I feel like I might be another rung on your ladder of grief, and that's okay if I am. I knew that might be the case going in, and it's been exciting, but I'm giving you your out."

"An out. That's what you're calling it?"

"That's what I'm calling it because that's what it is. I know you've been through a lot this year and maybe you've gotten yourself in too deep. I know how that feels and I worry that I'm part of that problem. This is your chance to think it through and cut me off, if that's what you want. I know I'm not the man you thought I was, but I want to be the man you need me to be."

He pauses, waiting for me to say something, but I'm speechless. It'll be a minute before it all sinks in.

Zayne reaches for my fingers and pulls them toward him. "I wish I could say that I'm detached from this decision, but the truth is I'm hopelessly dedicated to you and whatever you decide. I don't expect you to give me an answer tonight, or tomorrow even. Take all the time you need."

The crickets continue to shower me with noise, the darkness surrounding me while I stare down at him with a slack jaw. He's serious. He's actually looking for a commitment. I've been drowning my sorrows with liquor all night, scared to death by how his absence was making me feel and how I've ruined another woman's life, but he's not even married. Is this man for real?

All this anxiety and relief makes me light-headed, and I feel the world falling out from around me. I fall limply into Zayne's arms and he catches me.

"Clarisse." He lays me in the grass and moves the hair out of my eyes as I blink awake instantly, cherishing even this unusual moment we're sharing.

"You're not ready," he admits, kneeling next to me. "I shouldn't have forced you to dance with me. I shouldn't have pulled you away from your friends. God, damn it, I should know better." His fingers touch over my cheek and under my chin as he sighs. "You're still grieving. I should have turned you away that first night in my office. It was greed that stopped me from turning you away. I want you, Clarisse, but you need more time to heal. Hell, maybe you don't even want me back."

Our eyes clash. He couldn't have it more wrong. Is that why he thinks I've nearly passed out? Zayne helps me back to my feet and holds me gently. He makes sure I'm steady on my feet before letting me go.

"I want you, Clarisse. I think you know that. When you're ready to push aside the guilt and accept that Finlay was mentally unstable and you were doing the right thing—" His voice cuts off like he's struggling to remain composed. "There's nothing else you could have done."

We're not going there tonight. "Don't do that. Don't try and doctor me. His death is not what I'm hung up on right now."

"The lies. The fact that I'm not married." He thinks he knows.

I shake my head. "I don't care about that. I want to be with you, too."

That renders him silent and stunned. I take the opportunity to catch a breath and wipe away the spoiled emotions.

"I've wanted you for a while now, Clarisse. *Circumstances*," he emphasizes, "have kept us apart."

His thumb softly caresses my cheek. My eyes close when he tilts my head upwards. "I don't want to mess up those perfect, red lips," he whispers. "And when I kiss you, I don't want it to be forced by pride or despair. I don't want it to be because you're drunk and I'm depressed. I want it to be because you want me for me."

Another second passes with my lips begging for his kiss. I peek out of half-lidded eyes to see what the hold-up is, and huff, because I know now that he has no plans of kissing me tonight. I'm frustrated to say the least, but it's probably the smartest thing Zayne has done to date. If he kisses me now, it'll lead to other things, and we'll never be able to get back to this place again. I hate to admit it but he's right.

The words want to whip from my mouth, but Zayne stops me. He knows how difficult it is for me to trust him. How he knows, I don't understand, but his eyes show that he understands; and like that, I'm lost.

"It's okay," he answers. "One day soon we can be together and it'll mean something."

I'm still stunned that he'll even entertain a relationship with a cold-blooded killer. "Why, Zayne? Why are you the only one that doesn't look at me like I'm a murderer?"

"Because I refuse to believe that you are. I've dealt with a lot of crazies in my day, and you—my beautiful black widow—aren't one of them."

I'm entranced by his words and by the fact that he's not strong enough to spare me a kiss. He might secretly be the only good man I know. It's unfortunate that it has to be this way. He thinks I'm normal, that I wasn't born with the curse of mental instability. He thinks it's safe to get closer to me. You would think years of education in the field of psychology would have taught him a thing or two about women like me.

"How can you be so sure?" I warn him. "Bad things cling to me and I can't seem to shed the rotten luck."

"I can't be." He smirks at that admission and leans forward to kiss my cheek. "But at least I'll have you."

17: His Death Sentence

Many Moons Later

W e're in love Zayne and I, and although living with the man has been a bit trying, he's a good guy and works hard to make me happy. It takes effort to make our relationship work and I quickly learn that having a college crush and actually spending a lifetime with a person are two very different scenarios.

"Marry me," Zayne says, retrieving a sparkly silver thing from his pocket. "I know it sounds crazy, but I want to show you how much I love you and prove to you that we can live a long, happy life together, because you are not some arachnid entity that magically kills off her lovers."

I inwardly sigh. We've discussed this before. I'm not cut out to be his trophy wife. "You're already taking a chance on your life by inviting me into your home. You know the risk if you permanently accept me into your life, Zayne. I'll tell you that right now."

He lifts his chiseled chin and smirks. "I'll live."

The mischief in his eyes makes me want to believe him, but I'm not that naïve. "You think so."

He doesn't stand a chance.

He's not amused anymore, and that's just wonderful because I'm not trying to be funny.

"You're not cursed, Clare." His anger quickly burns off into a smile. "I'll prove it to you."

"And if you're wrong?"

"Then I'll die a happy man, knowing I gave you something worth living for, if only for a short while." He forces the dainty ring onto my finger.

He can be so darn cute sometimes, but I know in my heart that he's only doing this because he's afraid to be alone. "That's very sweet of you, Zayne, but are you sure about this? You've already been down this road before and look at where you landed. Besides, I've told you repeatedly that I can't be trusted. Do you really want to be linked to me and all my emotional baggage permanently?"

"Yes."

I hate his simple answers, but my scowl still manages to fade into a smile. "Have you listened to a single thing I've told you these past few months? I wasn't lying."

He smirks, analyzing me with his psychology degree like I'm some kind of pet project. "Honestly, Clare? I love you. I want to be with you, and I'm sure one day those horrible accusations will fade and you'll find a permanent place in your heart for me, right up there with those old memories, because that's all they'll be—memories."

"That's a morbid decision, lover." I crawl onto his lap and dangle my hands over his shoulders, smiling. It's his life. "I feel like I need to give you something in exchange for your death sentence."

His eyebrows pop up and down repeatedly, matching his mischievous smile. "There is this one other thing you can give me."

The look on his face has me thinking it's something sexual, but I soon learn I have him pegged so wrong this time. His palm smooths over my belly in a circular motion.

"You're joking." I twirl off of his lap, but he pulls me back onto him with a bear hug.

"I'm not." His voice growls in my ear as he continues to massage my flat belly like he's cherishing what's inside.

I struggle with the thought. While I've always dreamt of having a baby, and I've told him that, I never thought the crazy bastard would dare knock me up. "You don't mean that."

He smiles through my horror. "I do. And then we'll be a family for real. For that, I think I'd be willing to sit at number three."

"Three?"

"Baby. Then you. Then me. One. Two. Three."

I smile through the hurt as a tear trickles into the corner of my eye. I've taken a man's life. I have difficulty with the idea of bringing another little person into this screwy world. I lean backwards, so my head rests on Zayne's chest while he spoons me. I close my eyes. I don't deserve to bring another person into this world after taking someone so cruelly from it

Zayne instantly reads into my disparaging thoughts. "You're worth it."

It is true, I refuse to fully love Zayne the way I know I can, but a baby? Maybe he's right. That could be just the thing to make me feel whole again.

He will be the man to make me whole again.

18: Win, Lose, or Draw

Nine months later.

Zayne is standing behind me, rubbing my belly, the way he does every morning before he heads off to work. "How's my baby doing?"

"He's okay," I answer softly, convinced that we've been blessed with a healthy baby boy growing inside of me.

Smiling lips press against my neck. "I meant you, Clare. How are you feeling?"

"Good." *Surprisingly.* The first six months of pregnancy had been a nerve-wracking nightmare, but with each passing week things are better.

Now counting down the days left in my third trimester, I am in love. I'm in love with my child, in love with the gift that Zayne is giving me, and in love with the idea that I could actually give life and live a normal one myself, without the burden of my ex-lover dragging me under.

Life—as it is—is good.

I try to push away the self-conscious thoughts that plague me more and more the closer my due date gets, but nothing I try works. I feel huge, even though I've only gained about twenty pounds. I feel ugly, even though I don't have a double chin—yet! Zayne says he wants me, but ever since the baby started kicking, he acts like the idea of sex with me is taboo and disgusting. He says he still loves me just as much, but I need him to show me.

I steal his attention from the window. I see the way he notices that young blonde who jogs around the block repeatedly every morning before work, and I don't like it. I need him to look at me like that again. The silky strap of my loose nightie falls off my shoulder and exposes my swollen breast. He notices instantly and comes to me, his hand caressing the sensitive skin, his eyes meeting mine to make sure he's reading the situation right.

"Are you sure? You know what they say about making

love this close to your due date."

"For one, I don't believe it, but there's absolutely nothing wrong with a little sexual attention." I push the other thin strap off my shoulder, but my gown doesn't fall from my belly; it only rests there, framing my naked bust.

Zayne takes the hint and puts his mouth on me, sucking gently on a very erect nipple. It feels amazing, disguising the throbbing sensation in my chest. He gets carried away, and gives my breasts his thorough attention, just like I've been craving. Then he trails slow, wet kisses up my body, and he doesn't stop until he reaches my mouth.

"You're bad," he says, knowing I've conned him into getting turned on.

I smile and the rest is history. Zayne takes my hand and walks me to our master bedroom where he carefully makes love to each and every inch of my overgrown body. In moments like this, I know my stupid thoughts about Zayne cheating on me while he's out of town are ridiculous, even if this is the third weekend in a row he's had to leave me. I'm sure I'm just pulling these ideas out of thin air.

When he's finished with me, he caresses my stomach, gives it a kiss, and whispers a little secret to our baby.

I roll out of the bed. "Can you believe I'm only three days away from my due date?" I struggle to pull on my once loose-fitting clothes. They're now skin tight. I huff and even my baby boy recognizes how distraught I am. I take a deep breath and massage the cramp jabbing awkwardly at my side.

Zayne comes up behind me and replaces my hand with his, massaging the large lump that has to be Zayne Junior's butt jutting out. "You're beautiful, you know that right?"

"It's easier to believe that when you're here."

He wraps his arms around me. "I'll video call to see you and your baby bump as soon as my flight lands."

I pull away, feeling like an overinflated balloon. "I wish you could stay home."

"But you know I have to go."

"I know. It's just that baby Zayne is going to miss you so

much and maybe I will too."

He pulls me into a snug embrace. "What can I do to make you miss me less?" he asks, as if he didn't just do a damn good job pleasing me in our marital bed.

I think on it for a second. "Before you go, will you come for a short walk with me?" I know I should let him go—he really has to get going—but after nine long months, I'd like to spend these last few minutes holding his hand.

Although my feet are swollen, I look forward to getting out of the house. It's the least Zayne can do before he heads out for the weekend.

"Are you sure you should be hobbling around right now? Zayne Junior might fall out."

I slap at him and pucker my lips. Even with all these worries weighing on my mind, Zayne manages to make me smile.

"It's okay to take a day off," he insists.

"Zayne!" I plead. "The doctor said it's completely safe and healthy, as long as I'm not in any pain." I lift my hands and smile. "And I'm not."

He stares at me in disbelief and then pulls me into another hug. "Oh, Clare. I love you, babe."

"I know," I say softly, sinking into his arms.

He releases me long enough to pull out his runners. "How about that walk?"

My smile bursts from my mouth as I murmur to my belly. "Daddy's coming for a walk with us before noon. Take a picture, baby. This is a once in a lifetime kind of miracle."

"Whatever, Clare. I go for walks before noon."

"Oh, really? Name one time."

He thinks about it for longer than necessary. "Fine. Maybe I don't. But we walk."

My palms skim over his chest in a soothing manner. "I was only teasing you. I'm very happy that you're coming with us today. Thank you."

He leans down and kisses me thoroughly. "You're welcome but we'd better get out of here if I'm going to beat the heavy morning traffic."

I tremble when we first step outside. It can't be more than a minute past eight. The dew is still moist on the grass, and there's dampness in the air that causes Zayne to wrap his arm around my shoulder and huddle me against his side. I snuggle close, because I have a feeling this will be the last time he and I will be alone before the baby comes.

"I promise the second I get back, I'll rub this belly one last time and we can welcome our baby into this world together."

Zayne kisses my temple and holds me close. Even on this cloudy morning, I can feel his smile showering over me. I cherish the short moments like this one. Our quaint neighborhood in Forest Hills is peaceful at this time of day, and ever since Zayne chose me over his big-shot job, I like to forget how times are tough. With his ex-wife Casey raping him for every dollar he makes, it leaves little for us to survive on. Our mortgage eats up the bulk of our income, and I'm starting to wonder whether we'll ever be able to afford the new house we just moved into with the payments we're managing on our student loans.

Brushing all that aside, we walk down the quiet sidewalk, looking like the pregnant newlyweds that we are, hand in hand, lost in our own little world. I know I look overly round, and this pregnancy thing has done amazing things for my skin, but I don't feel particularly great today. I've been worrying a lot about Zayne's faithfulness lately.

I force myself to smile and keep up with his snail's pace, pushing through the pain of the recurring cramp in my side thanks to my overactive imagination. Exercise is important, I remind myself. If I want to birth a healthy baby boy, I need to keep up on my daily routine. I know Zayne hates my morning walks but he puts up with me. I tell him it's for the benefit of the baby and my sanity, and he won't ever deny me that.

We turn down a busier two-lane street, and I twirl out of his arm like his dance partner, still hanging on to his hand with my arm fully extended, the sound of traffic whooshing by me.

"Are you sure you have to go?" I ask, even though I know how it disappoints him when I make him feel guilty for supporting the family.

"I'm one of the newest employees and I don't have the luxury of turning this presentation down, Clare. We really need the money. You know I have to go."

This trip will take him back to San Francisco. How convenient for him. I know his brother lives there but I have a hard time believing that it's him he goes out with at night. I'm growing more furious by the second, but he's looking as handsome and happy as ever. If it was only about the job, I wouldn't be so angry inside. It's all the other crap he's not telling me about that pisses me off. He's probably thinking about all that adult fun right now. Why else would he be smiling when he's about to leave his pregnant wife for the weekend?

The block is alive with foot traffic, mostly dog-walkers and retired couples. Then there's that dumb blonde woman Zayne's always staring at. I pull my hand away from him, just barely breaking free because he doesn't want to release my fingers. I don't realize it's because I'm stumbling into the street without double checking for traffic.

The blonde woman darts into the street behind me. A speeding car swerves and just misses her, plowing into the curb lane, heading right in my direction. I'm so busy scowling at Zayne for watching the woman that I don't even know what's going on behind me until I hear the screeching tires.

"Clare, no!" Zayne shouts, witnessing everything.

First, our eyes connect. Then I watch his face contort into an ugly knot. It all happens so fast that there's no time for me to react. Zayne grabs for my wrist and pulls me past him with a violent tug. Time seems to move in slow motion as I twist around him. The speeding car clips my hip and sends me sailing onto the pavement. My hands skid across the ground, shredding the skin from my palms as the car doing all the damage pops the curb and rams into a security fence.

If I wasn't listening for his voice, I wouldn't have heard

the sickening crunching sound when Zayne's body hit the ground.

I want to scream, but my midsection is doing all the screaming for me. My chin jerks upwards, working desperately to pull air into my lungs. I can't see my husband, but I can hear commotion all around me. Everything is blurry for a moment. I hear a high-pitched ringing sound in my ears, brakes screeching, and drivers shouting. My eyes swing over to the people across the street who are frozen in horror.

They aren't looking at me.

I have to see how bad it is. I use all my strength to drag myself across the pavement. My legs are numb and my arms feel like wet noodles, but I'm moving in the direction of everyone's attention. I need to hear his voice. I have to know he's okay; this while dark red blood saturates my own shirt and gushes between my legs. I force myself to my feet, holding my bloody, aching belly.

"Zayne!" I scream, begging for him to answer me.

More cars brake in a domino effect, the screech of their tires a repetitive sound that almost deafens me. It doesn't take long for the street to pile up with parked vehicles and the sidewalk with bewildered pedestrians. Drivers farther down the line begin shouting abuse in an accusatory way, opening up their windows and waving angry hands; if they only knew how ignorant they were being.

I'm fucking dying here!

I limp around the damaged car between me and Zayne, holding the gash in my side, glaring at the woman whimpering on the curb who has removed her earbuds long enough to realize what she's done. An elderly gentleman is tending to her, but the blonde's body remains fully intact. In that moment, she looks up at me. I will never forget her selfish face as I search for my reason for living.

I squeeze my eyes shut as I stagger around the car, my eyes instantly flashing to the bloody mess on the pavement. I see it with my own two eyes. Vomit pools in my throat as the image of my husband's lifeless body pinned beneath the tire of the car is permanently etched into my brain.

"Noooooo!" I howl at the suddenly dark, cloudy sky.

I crash to my knees, landing in a puddle of my own blood, where I succumb to my nervous breakdown. Starved of sanity, I skip a breath and pass out in front of the injured driver who murdered my husband and unborn child.

19: Life or Death

Loud clapping sounds jolt me out of a warm safe place in my mind. I wake to a police officer snapping his fingers in front of my face. "She's awake," he shouts as two paramedics lift me up and strap me onto a board.

No matter what they do to slow the bleeding of my midsection, it doesn't help. All I see is one bandage after another absorbing what's left of my blood.

One man looks to the other. "We're leaving—now."

I despise the way the uniformed man looks at me. I see the pity behind his eyes. I want to claw those eyes out.

I know. My baby's not going to make it, and, yes, I saw how my husband's life ended, too. If I thought life had ever been cruel to me before, I was wrong.

I slip away for a few minutes, but everything slowly reappears when my eyes blink open. I'm indoors now. Florescent lights blind me from above while emergency professionals continue work on me like I'm not even there.

Hello! I can hear you, assholes.

I start to wonder what it'd be like to not be here as I drift in and out of consciousness. It feels as though I've ejected my uterus, but I hear the voices reminding me that there will be an emergency delivery in the very near future.

"This woman is pregnant!" a nurse shouts.

"The baby! It's in distress," another announces. "She has to deliver this thing now."

It.

Thing.

Don't they understand that this *thing* is my own flesh and blood? Another stab of pain strikes my midsection, and it feels like I'm being split in two. I bend forward, moaning through the pain, wrestling against the restraints.

"My baby!" rips from my throat.

One of the paramedics finally acknowledges that they're working on a human being. "How long has she been having contractions?"

Just as the pain becomes too much to handle, I feel my arm being pricked, and a cold fluid runs into my veins. My eyes flutter shut, and I must fade out for a while. When I reopen my eyes, I'm in a pale yellow room, lying on a delivery table, with my lower half bare and my legs split apart. I roll my head to see whether I'm alone and, as I try to close my legs to loosen the pressure there, a nurse pries my legs even farther apart.

"Welcome back," she says with a husky tone, and an irritating blend of sweetness and surprise. "My name is Linda. I'm here to help you. Anything you need, just say it."

"What's going on?" I moan, hoping they've already extracted my poor baby. Talking takes more effort than I expected, causing pain to sear my middle. "Ahh!" I cry out.

"You're about to deliver this baby. We were hoping you'd come to in time to meet your little guy. Give me a push," Linda grunts, like a football player.

"What? I don't fucking think so!" I'm afraid I might push out my spleen. My middle is wrapped in clean bandages, but I can just imagine the horror show hiding beneath them.

I become lightheaded from thinking too hard and have to press my eyes shut to get through the next contraction. A monitor starts to beep erratically. I wonder if I'm having a heart attack.

"Shit!" Linda shouts. "Go get the doc! Code pink. Code pink!"

A young girl takes off running, panicking doubly as much as the larger nurse.

Gasping from the pain ripping at my crotch, my voice croaks, "Code pink?" I have no idea what the hell that means, but by the urgency of the nurses rushing in the door, I know it isn't good.

A tall, middle-aged woman, who I presume is the doctor, casually appears at my bedside. The nurse quickly exchanges places with her and grabs onto my hand. Words are exchanged but it's not any language I can seem to understand. I wait for Linda to explain to me what code pink means, but instead she looks away to monitor one of the machines while she turns down the alarm. I hear her take a deep breath before looking back to me.

"On this next contraction, I need you to push. The baby's come too far to turn back now. Push like your life depends on it."

Is there a chance my baby's life does? There's no way he survived that hit. Is there?

Linda looks me right in the eyes with a solemn expression on her face. "This is it, Clarisse. In three-two-one, push!" she shouts, forcing me to clench my teeth and scream with all that I have to deliver my baby boy.

"Ah. Ah. Ah," the doctor warns, playing with my bloodied bandage.

"No more pushing!" Linda shouts, like she's my lifelong coach.

"I have to push," I cry. It hurts so much. My stomach heaves and contracts uncomfortably, urging my baby forward.

"No you don't," Linda informs me. "You're not contracting."

"I think my body knows when I have to push, and I have to push!" I shout, giving it another shot. But nothing new happens, and no matter how hard I try, nothing changes.

The doctor takes a long tool from the young nurse. My eyes burst out of their sockets.

"Relax. They're just forceps. This will all be over in a minute."

The second she flips my baby, I feel his head ripping me open. His body follows with another agonizing push. I feel the very second my baby boy is pulled free from my body, and I notice how the room falls silent.

Dead silent.

The nurses work together, urgently caring for my baby boy. Why won't they show me his face? Why isn't anyone talking? "Why isn't he crying?" So many questions and no answers.

The only sound is the quick movements of the

emergency personnel as they cut the umbilical cord and pass my baby off to a machine. They're trying to revive him. Who are they kidding? He's already dead.

I settle back on the bed as my eyelids absorb the tears that are building for a storm. I hear a commotion. My eyes shoot across the room. A storm of nurses rush toward the door with my baby boy. I see him. His skin... it's pale and bluish, with patches of blood smeared across his little baby body. His head is covered in a swirl of dark hair like his father's.

"My baby," I cry, reaching out to him.

I suck in an emotional breath. Tears drip from the corners of my eyes. My breaths become quick and labored. I roll my head back, my sight becoming blurry again. There's no way I'm going to survive this. "That's our baby."

Zayne's baby boy.

My voice is scratchy and slurred when I speak. "Where are they taking my baby?"

The large nurse stands before me and connects with my watery gaze. "I'm sorry, Clarisse. They've just taken him to the room next door. Our machine wasn't charging properly. I promise that you can see him in a minute."

"I don't understand. What's wrong with my son?"

Linda knows I don't actually want the answer—I'm in no shape to hear it—but she tells me anyway. "I'm supposed to wait for the doctor to tell you this, but I'm afraid your baby's not going to make it."

"What?" I shake my head from side to side. "No!"

"He wasn't breathing."

I grab on to the nurse's turquoise scrubs and pull her violently toward me. "I just lost my husband. I need that child. He's all I have left. Don't you dare tell me he's going to die."

I let the lady go and watch her eyes bug out from her face while she tries to straighten herself.

"He was really active last night," I explain. "I could feel him rolling around this morning. He was fine."

The woman turns her eyes to the floor and clasps her

hands together, as if in casual prayer. "That was before the accident."

I see the way she keeps her distance from the bed now, and she's lucky. I'm ready to snap. She busies herself around the room but makes no move to check on me again until the doctor returns to finish what she started.

"Doctor, I don't need any more of these bullshit lies. I just lost my husband. My baby's not breathing. Tell me what's going on here!"

I can't even shed my tears, as my stomach convulses again. Before she can speak, I fold forward in pain. It feels like another baby is about to grace us with its presence.

"What's happening?" I cry.

Linda takes my hand and smiles somberly. "It's your placenta. This shouldn't hurt, but you need to be still."

"Ready?" the doctor asks me, hovering at the end of my bed. "And push!" she urges.

I don't want to push, I really don't, but the force of the contraction makes me do it. Right when I start to wonder whether it'll ever end, I deliver a bloody placenta.

The doctor rolls it around in her hands, examining it. Who the hell knows what she's looking for? As if this day hasn't been nightmarish enough, now I have to watch a woman molest my bloody insides.

"Why won't you bring me to my baby?" I howl, rolling my head backwards.

The doctor drops my innards into an aluminum tray and returns between my legs, doing her best to touch up my battered body, while the nurse coos to me. "It won't be long now. We'll get you fixed right up."

Everything from my tits down is numb—numb and yet throbbing, like one big blister set to explode.

With a disturbing feeling rolling through my exhausted body, I cry to myself. "My baby."

It's hard to find a breath after all that exhaling, but even more so when the young nurse appears in the doorway empty-handed. I wait for her to explain what's happening, but she hesitates. She glances at the nurse next to me and shakes her head, announcing in a small voice, "I'm sorry."

Linda tries to touch my hand, but with my last ounce of energy and my last shred of sanity, I swipe my arm away from her. I nearly smack her cheek in the process, just barely breezing by the curly hair sprouting from the oversized mole on her chin.

"You're sorry? You're sorry for what?" My voice rises and I snap completely.

The young nurse looks like she wants to scurry off.

"We're sorry for your loss," Linda says.

"You mean for my husband, right? The loss of my husband." I grab at my side and my hand sinks into the soggy bandage. I glance toward the door and catch the undeniable shake of the nurse's head.

"Why is she shaking her head?"

I already know the answer, but I refuse to accept it. If she were a little closer to the bed I might have wrung her neck. From across the room, I imagine squeezing the breath right out of her throat until the life drains from her eyes the way mine has.

The doctor stays at the foot of my bed. Another nurse finally enters the room to deliver her the official news. She holds a swaddled baby out to the doctor—my baby. He looks just like his father, too. Full lips, dark lashes, and a swatch of obsidian hair.

The doctor stands there in place with her downturned eyes closing. In her arms is a bluish baby swaddled in a white blanket. Saddened eyes touch mine from across the bed. She comes toward me quickly and holds the swaddled baby out to me. "He didn't make it, Clarisse."

20: Under the Influence

The last thing I remember is warmth washing over me like a tidal wave and a scream that echoes indefinitely in my ears. The room starts to spin. The searing pain in my side lessens after I feel a sharp prick in my thigh. The sound of the doctor's mouth moving next to my ear blends into a blur of streaming color, right before the room is swallowed in darkness.

I have no idea how much time passes, but I wake dressed with fresh bandages, there's a clean hospital gown on my back, and I'm lying in a small bed propped up a good distance from the floor. Still, the room is quite dark, and without the heavy blinds cracked open, I can't tell whether it's morning, noon, or night. I don't know how I got here, but I know one thing: I'm alone and scared.

Is this hell?

No. In the darkness, I can picture my smiling husband, the way he gazes into my eyes, wraps his arms around my pregnant body, and massages my baby bump. He tells me he loves me. No. This is not hell. This is life.

As soon as my eyes adjust to the darkness, I glance around the sterile, shadowed room, noticing how tightly I'm tucked into the bed. A phone starts buzzing next to me, and my eyes scatter around the room before landing on the white thing sitting on the machine at my bedside. I barely have to lean over to reach it, but I feel that strain everywhere. I lift the receiver and notice it has two buttons and no cord. I hold the phone close to my face, staring at the green button and press it.

I wait for someone to whip open my door now that I've awakened, but nothing changes. "Hello?" I answer, barely recognizing my own scratchy voice.

"Oh, good. You're awake." The woman starts rambling at ninety miles an hour, and it all goes in one ear and out the other. "I'm sorry," is the last thing she says, and it's the only thing I here.

"Who is this?" I ask, the air whooshing out of my mouth.

"Clarisse, it's Brenda—your mother-in-law."

Monster-in-law, to be exact. Zayne always finds a way to point that out whenever Brenda calls for something. She never much liked me, except for the drama I brought to her family. She loves drama more than her own flesh and blood. She barely cared when I would call to tell her about Zayne's accomplishments.

Zayne. Everything comes back to me like a tsunami to the head. Sensations push and pull at my brain strings. *The way Zayne holds me and cherishes our unborn child in my belly. The nighttime snuggles. The morning smiles. The lingering kisses. The speeding traffic. The ignorant jogger. The blood. The baby.* Exhaustion swoops over me, ripping me from my reverie.

"I've been trying to reach you for days," Brenda says. "I'm so sorry, but we had to. We didn't know how long you would be out of commission for and we couldn't wait any longer. The rest of the family was up from Alabama. We were all in mourning. We needed that closure."

I'm shaking my head, a horrific look covering my face, but she can't see that. "You had to do what?" I whisper.

"Lay my son to rest—bury him. Zayne was buried this morning."

Tears pierce my eyes, and the floor falls out from beneath me. I have to suck in a breath to keep the cry from erupting through the room like an earthquake.

"We waited and waited. Believe that we waited," Brenda says. "But we didn't know when you'd wake up. What do you know? You're awake!" she says like it's a good thing.

I'd rather be dead.

They couldn't have waited twenty-four hours for me to recover from the loss of my baby? Brenda couldn't mind her own fucking business, allow me to make the arrangements and attend my own husband's funeral? What about what Zayne wanted? He never wanted to see the ground, locked away in a wooden box for all eternity. He was a free soul and wanted to be set loose in the mountains, and now I'm fucking furious. As the tears subside, I fear for the woman on the other end of the phone.

"We're staying at your house," she continues. "I didn't figure you would mind, since you're laid up and all."

I don't speak. With closed eyes, I choke back my tears of fury. Is this my punishment for all the ways I've wronged people over the years?

"The funeral was beautiful, in case you wondered," Brenda says, filling my silence. "The casket was beautiful. So many colleagues and students came to pay their respects. It was a grand affair. Casey stood next to his casket in your place. She's pretty shaken up about this. You really should have been there."

I speak through gritted teeth. "I would have been there if you had waited." I pause for a much needed breath. "This is my husband we're talking about—mine!"

"Yes, dear. *My* son. The love of Casey's life. Who else would I be talking about?"

Patience was never my strong suit, but this woman plucks at my last straw. "Zayne didn't want to be buried; you know that, Brenda."

She fluffs my emotions off. "Oh, that's nonsense. No one in our family is cremated."

"Get the fuck out... of *my* house," I state angrily before wheeling the phone clear across the room. The plastic thing makes a hefty dent in the drywall before it clatters onto the floor in three pieces. I cry inconsolably for as long as I can handle, clutching at the pain in my side, until my mind drifts away from all this mental anguish and defeat. I feel like I'm transposed into an alternate reality where I live in darkness, but my life is in my own hands, and I control karma like the Black Widow herself.

21: Karma

I missed my own husband's funeral. It's no wonder I've become so irrational. I'm angry at the world. All this new pain leaves me feeling numb and pretty helpless in a society full of careless maniacs. Post-partum depression hits me like a sledge-hammer colliding with a brick wall, but the hospital staff can only keep me there for so long. When Zayne's limited insurance runs out, I leave the hospital against doctor's orders and call a cab to take me home.

It takes me a few minutes to get out of the waiting cab, but I do it on my own. I walk with a painful limp to the front door of my home and drop my bag there. I look down at my welcome mat, instantly getting choked up. Zayne brought that mat home to me on our first day in our new place. He called it our first house-warming present. That doesn't even touch how we picked out this huge house because it was the perfect place to raise our family.

I breathe deeply and check over my shoulder. The car in the driveway tells me that one of his family members has hung around despite my graphic warning days ago to get the hell out. I wonder which one of them has the gall to stick around and deal with me after all I've been through.

I reach for the door handle, but it's locked. I consider ringing the doorbell, but this is my house. I rummage through my purse for a key, but it's not there. Angered by this, I punch my finger into the doorbell repeatedly and then start banging on the door. My heart beats more erratically by the second. I know I really shouldn't get worked up like this, but panic takes me before the door whips open. Standing inside my home is a man, maybe a few years younger than Zayne, with the same chestnut eyes and dark lashes.

"Whoa there. Can I help you?" he says before checking to see who it is.

What the hell is *he* doing in my home?

I shove my way past him, slapping both my hands against his shirtless chest. With a groan, I hobble into the front room. Zayne's brother follows me quickly, like I've somehow invaded *his* privacy. I spin around to berate him and grab at my side when a searing pain wraps around my waist.

"What the hell are you doing here?" My voice loses its gusto by the time I get the entire sentence out.

"I—uh—I just—"

I hold a flattened palm out to his clean-shaven face and move toward the kitchen. I stop and gasp when I enter the room. For me to have hoped that he was looking after my house while I was in hospital is a delusion. Dirty pots and pans are heaped in not one, not two, but three piles on the counter next to the dishes piled up in the kitchen sink.

"What's that smell?" I ask, turning to face the shirtless man standing behind me.

He raises his eyebrows, not knowing how to answer me. His dimples wink at me, even while he wears a frown.

"Parker?" I ask again, not waiting for an answer. Maybe it's the rotten food sticking to the pans, or maybe it's because he forgot to take the garbage out for the past week. "You just thought you would raid my cabinets and leave the mess for who... the maid?"

Anyone who knows Zayne and me, knows we don't have a fucking maid. Maybe, if Parker would have visited once in a lifetime, he would know that.

I continue to scowl at the younger and taller version of my late husband. I would have thought that Parker, being a cop for a big city police department, would have learned how to show an ounce of remorse, or at least know when to fake it, but he doesn't. The look on his face, I would say, is smug.

"Get out of my house!" I scream with all that I have.

Parker decides to start with silence as I follow him back to the living room. He retrieves a T-shirt from the back of the sofa and throws it over his shoulder, followed by a black duffle bag. "I figured I would stay here and help you get back on your feet, since it's a big empty house and you're all alone; but it's okay. I'll get out of your hair."

I don't bother answering him. I figure the less I say, the quicker he'll leave.

"Look, for what it's worth, I'm really sorry for your loss."

I nod, hinting for him to move along in the nicest way possible. Zayne always said that his brother was a man of few words, but Parker can't seem to shut his mouth around me.

He turns back. "I'm sorry you had to learn how rotten my mother can be, too. It's not right that you had to miss your own lover's funeral."

All thoughts but one comes screaming to the front of the conversation. I look up at Parker with the meanest eyes I can conjure. "He was my husband!" I snap, pointing toward the door.

He finally takes the hint and exits my house, leaving me with a pile of housework and boatload of personal baggage to clean up on my own. I cross the living room slowly and then fling the box of half-eaten pizza off the coffee table in a fit of anger and frustration. I kick the used blankets off my sofa and drop onto it, expelling a long breath before crumbling into myself and crying.

I suffer through a long bout of tears that involves me blaming everyone but Zayne for what has happened, and then I stare at the wall. Staring off into space is dangerous, but I do it for a long, long time, drowning myself in grief and helplessness. How can simply being alive be this painful?

My daydreams collide with reality. I'm at a loss for what is real anymore. My hand slides over the phantom kick in my stomach, but it's almost as if a baby had never set up shop there. I try looking around my house, but it's painful; everything reminds me of what will never be. Resting my eyes is no better, for every time I close my eyes, I see him. I see blood. I see that blonde woman jogging, a swerving vehicle, death; I'm finding it hard to maintain my sanity. I try to focus on what is real. There's me. Then there's Zayne's asshole brother.

A knock at the door pulls me from my thoughts. I stand at the door but make no move to open it.

"I know you're there," Parker says through the door.

He carries on with his *I'm sorry* this and *I'm sorry* that. Inside, I'm like: *Will you stop fucking saying that?* I've had enough of it—enough.

With eyes shining with unshed tears, I lock my front door. My eyes whip back and forth. I have to keep Parker out. I struggle with the heavy wardrobe next to the door. After a couple of grunts and a sharp pain in my side, I get it to slide in front of that door. I might have gouged the wood floor in the process, but Parker won't be coming back in now. I laugh, but there's no humor in it. I think I've lost my mind.

Parker's shouting for me to let him in, but I ignore him. He follows me from window to window and watches me close him out of my life. I go to reach for the next curtain but instead hunch over in pain.

"You can try to shut me out, Clarisse," he says, his voice steady and clear, "but I'm not leaving until I know you're okay."

I limp around the house to finish the job, hurting my recovery but managing to pull closed all the heavy drapes with a swift whoosh of fabric in every direction. I keep at it, until I've blocked all light from breaching my depressing home. I shuffle toward the front of the house and settle against the rustic hall table Zayne got me for my birthday.

Once I'm satisfied that his brother's left me alone, I head for the master bedroom. I ignore the fucking mess on my way and swing the door open like I might find someone standing there on the other side. I don't. The room is as we left it before the accident—*we*. I freeze in a momentary lapse of memory.

Zayne's side of the bed is made and mine is a mess. His old man slippers are resting at the foot of the bed, right where he always leaves them. It looks like he's gone for the day, as if he might actually return home at some point. But he's not going to return. Not this time. He's gone for fucking good.

I rush the bed, rip the sheets away maniacally, and throw them to the floor. I kick his slippers under the bed, my panic-stricken scream echoing through the empty room while I pull at my mussed up hair. Moments later, when I realize what I've done—disturbed the last piece of Zayne's existence—fear grips me. He's not coming back. I'm alone again. Again. I'm always so fucking alone.

Wearing a vacant expression, I crawl back onto the stripped bed, lie on my side, and clutch on to Zayne's pillow for dear life. I squeeze it and inhale the lingering scent. He's not completely gone from my life. Not yet, no. No. No! He can't be.

Another disturbing sound leaves my mouth, that wail echoing through my empty house. I don't remember breathing. I don't remember night falling. I don't remember ever leaving the bed, letting go of that pillow, or getting to my feet. I only remember that large, gentle hand on the small of my back, leading me to my guest bedroom; that same man pulls open the blankets and offers me a hesitant shoulder to cry on.

Parker wraps an arm around my shoulder and lets me cry all over him, until the front of his grey T-shirt is soaked through with my tears. His only escape is to answer the door for the woman with the pills that will fix it all.

I hear mumbling in the living room, but I'm too deeply lost in my own head to make out the words. All I know for sure is that one second Parker's leaving me and the next he's hovering over my bed with a concerned expression wrinkling his forehead.

"I can't take it anymore, Parker," I whisper, feeling physically and emotionally spent. "They're not coming back. There's nothing left for me here."

"It's okay, Clarisse. Take these." He takes my hand and drops two pills into my palm. "The doctor said it'll help you feel better."

I blindly do as he says from that day forward, sipping from the glass in his hand, living in a heavy, drug-induced fog, spending the best part of my days under the sheets with my eyes pinched shut, alone. Days pass and then weeks. I don't remember opening and closing my door. I barely remember getting up to go to the bathroom. I don't eat much, but when I do it's a bite or two from the plate that keeps materializing on my nightstand.

Then one day, he's gone. The plate I had been picking from is gone. The glass of water and bottle of pills, gone. The room is dark and shadowed, the blinds drawn tightly shut, reminding me only of my nights: long, lonely, and quiet—a battle that knows no borders.

There's a pounding at my front door. I slowly move toward the loud, obnoxious sound, noticing how my hip protests only momentarily. Where the wardrobe once rested in front of my door to the outside world, I see the floor is now void of furniture. I can't remember the last time I washed my hair, and I certainly am not expecting company.

I peer through the peephole, and a ghostly figure of the man I married is standing there. I gasp for a breath and shake my head to register my thoughts. I blink hard and look again, only to find that it's Parker standing there. My eyes settle on his tired chestnut eyes, trimmed with those dark eyelashes. I can't stop staring at him.

Is he back here to make me feel this way? Where I remember his face being clean-shaven the last time I had a look at him, he's now wearing a five o'clock shadow. He's dressed in a fancy, black suit that looks a lot like the one Zayne wore for our wedding. I don't think I should open the door.

"Go away." My voice is but a croak from lack of use.

Parker raises his eyebrows in a look of determination. "I'm not going anywhere without you. We've only got an hour."

Pressing my forehead against the door, I beg him. "Please. Just leave me alone."

After a moment of silence and a prayer, I peer through the peephole again. He's still standing there and, as if he knows that I'm watching him, he moves one of his eyes close to the hole, his hands framing his face. I feel violated by the intimacy of it.

"You missed their funerals, Clarisse. I'm not going to let you miss your baby's memorial service, too. My mother agreed to hold off the service for this long. Three months was the best I could do."

My baby's memorial service? Why is this the first time I'm hearing of this?

"Clarisse. I know you're still there. You need to get out of this house before you drive yourself crazy."

I huff, in a mixture of frustration and sadness. "It's a bit late for that, I'd say." I pause to think about it for a second. "I'm not coming."

I spin around and walk away, scooping up a bottle of pills that can only be the ones I've been living off of lately. I find comfort in the idea of taking all of them right now to knock myself out. Yes, I think skipping today is a great idea. I'll try again tomorrow.

I hear a jiggling of my front door knob, and I scurry to my guest bedroom. I tell myself that no one can get to me here, but then the lock slides free and my front door creaks open.

"Clarisse, I'm coming in," Parker says in warning. "I won't let you do this. You've hidden yourself away for long enough. It's time to face the world." He lets himself inside the house.

I place the bottle on the nightstand and kneel next to it, shaking my head when I see that there are only two lonely pills in the bottle I thought would save me. "No," I shout back to him. "I don't think it's time. You need to leave."

"It's time, Clarisse," Parker says, twisting the door knob and pushing open the guest bedroom door.

I jump up out of surprise and look at him through wide eyes. He stands in the doorway of my room, but the way he leans against the doorframe is much too familiar. When he looks up at me with those eyes, it slays me, nearly taking me back to my knees.

"Please," I beg, my heart aching in a way I'd like to forget.

"Do I really have to say it again? I'm not leaving without you."

I swallow from the depth of his promise. "You most certainly are." If I can just get him out of the doorway, I can lock him out and I'll be set.

I step toward him, and he stands up to his full height again, but when I push on the door in an attempt to close it between us, his shoe stops it from getting closure.

"Nice try, but it's not going to work. Get dressed," he says. "I'm not going anywhere."

I huff again. Parker is just as persistent as Zayne was. At this rate, I have to believe I'll be rid of him faster if I give in. "Fine!" I shout, making it known that I'm not going with him because I want to.

He smiles softly and backs away at the same time as I do. "I'll wait for you here." He glances at the floor from the hall, but he doesn't trust me enough to step any farther away.

So much for my last ditch attempt at getting him out of the room. I can see this is a fight I won't win, so I open up the closet. The black dress I thought I'd find buried at the back is hanging in front of the other out-of-season clothes, with a pair of black nylons strung around the neck of the hanger. My favorite black heels are piled up on the floor beneath it.

I know I didn't do this myself, but I refuse to admit how *out of it* I've been lately, so I put myself together and act like nothing is out of the ordinary.

Parker follows me to the bathroom. "I don't get why you're forcing me to leave my house and publicly grieve my child. You're pretty messed up, you know that?"

The quirk of his eyebrow rejects my question and throws it back at me. "It's for the best."

I leave the bathroom door half open. I'm not in the mood to argue with him anymore. I strip naked right in front of him and catch his eye before he quickly looks away. I ignore him some more and take a quick shower. He turns away long enough to respect my privacy while I exit the tub and dress.

While I towel dry my hair, I take a peek at him. I want to strangle his handsome throat. This was not in my plans for today, or ever for that matter. At least he doesn't hassle me about how his mother has titled this event a celebration of Zayne Junior's life—the child who won't ever get to have a single birthday let alone have a life worth celebrating. I clench my teeth together, to fight off the emotions.

I don't know if I can do this.

I don't want to see Zayne's family. I'm not ready to say goodbye to him yet. It hurts too much to think about my baby boy.

I smooth my hands down the front of my dress. It fits like a glove over my now flat stomach. I cringe while I throw a few things into a black handbag and walk back to the guest bedroom. I pull on my shoes and sigh.

Parker finally trusts that I'm coming and heads for the front foyer. I follow him and stop in front of the mirror hanging on the wall. I don't recognize the woman staring back at me. She's unsightly, with black rings under her eyes and red blotchy cheeks. My hair. Ugh. There's no way I can wear it down, so I rake it into a messy bun atop my head, knowing it's the best I can do right now.

When I step out of the house, panic takes me. I gasp for breath and stare at that damn welcome mat beneath my heels.

I don't think I can do this.

Parker comes to my rescue, grabs on to my elbow, and lifts me until I'm standing upright again. "Are you okay?"

"I can't—" I start, but telling him I can't breathe is futile.

The fact that he gets me moving toward his car in a matter of a minute is a miracle, but I refuse to get in that death trap. Not only can I not do this, but I don't want to, either. "I can't," I say softly.

He looks around, but he doesn't find an answer. "The cemetery is too far away to walk, Clarisse. I get that you're upset, but you're safe with me. I promise I'll drive carefully."

I shake my head and tears start to resurface in my eyes.

I'm not ready for this.

He practically carries me the rest of the way to his car. "Oh, yeah, that reminds me." He pulls open the driver's side door, ducks into the backseat, and comes out with a nifty looking cap. It's black and lacy, with an opaque sheet of black fabric draped from it. "It's a veil," he says, as if I couldn't figure it out for myself. "It's for a widowed woman in mourning."

"I know what it is, Parker."

He shrugs his shoulders. "Everyone's calling you the Black Widow, so I thought it would be suiting." He props it haphazardly on the side of my head, and the fabric falls over my sunken eyes. "Honestly, I thought you'd want to hide your face from people in general. There's no need to show everyone all your shit. Am I right?"

I check my reflection in his car window. "Thank you." I adjust it a bit, and in all honesty, it doesn't look half bad. If nothing else, it gives me a wall to hide behind. That's step one. Step two is convincing Parker to take the bus. Easily done. He must understand why I'm so hesitant to get in his car, but I doubt he knows he's agreed to an indirect route to the cemetery.

I can't risk traveling past the scene of the accident, even if months have passed and Zayne's blood has been washed from the sidewalk.

Dressed all in black, I board the city bus. Parker follows closely behind me. I make a point of not looking at him; he looks so much like Zayne. It's painful to watch the depth of my sorrow reflected in those eyes.

I stare blankly out the window until we arrive at the cemetery. I accept Parker's elbow and get off the bus. Together, we pass through the iron gate, and glide through the grass toward the gathering of people. A big, black bird squawks, perched in a tree high above me. I glance upward and shield two rays of sunshine with a hand, squinting into the canopy of trees from beneath the sheer black veil. After a moment of searching for the cause of the noise, I drop my hand and give in to my insecurities—eyes watching me, pecking at me like vultures.

Everyone stares—and by everyone, I mean every last person in attendance whose name is not Parker. A few people gasp; I'm not sure who, because I refuse to make eye contact with any of them. Out of the corner of my eye, I catch Parker's mother waving for us to join her, but I also catch a glimpse of Zayne's ex-wife next to her. *Yeah, I don't think* so. The fact that Casey is even here—like she has any relation to my baby—just murders my self-control. I let out a whimper I can't hold in.

Parker flexes his bicep, tucking me closer to his side. I hang my head in shame. A grey fog settles in, swooping around me and threatening to pull me away to that faded place I like to stay.

Parker and I both turn our chins away from the others and slump our shoulders, standing to the side of the church minister who is about to perform the service. Although I remember specifically requesting a non-religious ceremony, the first words out of the man's mouth are about God. The man raises his hands and looks up into the sky as he speaks, like my child is up there. Who knows, maybe he is.

"It looks like God needed another flower for his garden."

People nod their heads and share smiles. My eyes dart from one sucker to the next. Rather than making a scene, screaming that *God should try birthing his own damn flowers*, I close my eyes and listen with an open, broken heart.

"We have come together this morning to remember Zayne Junior—to mourn the loss of a loved one so small he has not even had a moment to grow into a memory. Rather, we mourn the empty spaces in a home that has been prepared for his arrival. We mourn for the loss of hopes not realized, and we mourn for the opportunities he will not have: to catch his first snowflake on his tongue, to dip his toes into the ocean, or bury his feet in white sand."

The man's voice falters when he reaches for the canvas draped with a black fabric. My eyes flash forward. No one told me there would be a photograph. I told them no photographs. Please tell me there were not pictures taken of my baby. The minister pulls away the dull black fabric, and my eyes latch on to that image like magnetic lasers. A baby—full grown and perfect—with skin too pale and lips too pink, but it's the swirl of obsidian hair atop his head that brings the tears.

"To the family who will never see baby's first smile, first step, or first anything. We will never see baby Zayne wrapped in his mother's arms, or playing catch with his late father. We will never see him grow up. We can only remember that he was a gift from a gracious God, and God has decided that his time has come."

The minister's voice is unwavering and grows louder to overcome the dramatic sobs from the small crowd. Other family members listen, weep, and carry on, wiping their tears with a tissue or hugging the person beside them. I remain locked away in my own head—my own hell—paralyzed by the grief that has been festering there.

"We cannot shed tears over a child we have not known, but we can shed tears with his surviving mother. Let us pray for her in her time of sorrow. May we join together to push through the sadness and conflict, from the loss of this new life, and together we shall find peace in this sorrow and grief."

Parker takes my hand and clutches it tightly. I look up at him, and he looks right back at me, his eyes sharing the same grief as my own. Our eyes hook in a moment of deep understanding and sadness, and it is then our hearts bind in a permanent and shared torment.

The minister gives us that moment, lowers his voice, and then takes both of my hands into his. "Do not let the death of this child be in vain. We can be certain that he is now with his father, and our Father."

His words stake my heart. It's both distasteful and distressing for me to have to be put through this service when Brenda knows full well I was raised in a non-religious family. Still, I tolerate it. I can respect the relief it gives those who whole-heartedly believe in forgiveness. I take a deep breath and blow it out to steady the rapid beat of my heart. Parker moves closer to me in a show of support, standing next to me like the foundation to my wall.

The service wraps up quickly. One-by-one people approach me, shake my hand, and pull me into a hug I don't ask for. The only reason I endure it is because Parker stands by my side the entire time and moves people along. I'm thankful when the last woman in line, whom I've never met before, takes my hand. She looks at the large framed photograph of my deceased baby and then at me.

"The death of a child is the most devastating loss. I'm so sorry."

I suffer through the rest of the afternoon surrounded by a bunch of people I barely know and many I've never seen before in my life. I accept the fresh-cut flower Parker hands to me; it's stained blue like my baby's skin. I tilt my head down, consumed by tears, loneliness, and heartache.

The reassuring words shared by the man everyone's calling *Father* are depressing enough; I don't need to hear the whispers. Some people are selfish, insincere, and just plain cruel. Two older ladies standing next to me don't even bother to offer me their condolences. They have age and life written all over their faces, and yet they show no sign of remorse for their lack of sympathy.

Parker notices I'm in distress and collects me in his arms, but that just makes them whisper more.

That's the Black Widow right there.

I heard she killed her last two husbands.

It looks like she's going to do Parker in next.

"Ignore them," Parker mumbles to me, and I do.

I'll leave it up to my dear sister Karma to settle up with them later. Based on their ages, I expect it won't be long at all.

22: Those Little Things

I remain silent for a long time after the memorial service. I'm quiet for the rest of the afternoon and all the way home. On the bus, Parker offers me a strong shoulder to cry on, but I turn it away. That will only make things worse. It's not until we reach my driveway that I finally speak to him again.

"Why the photographs, Parker? You don't share photos of a stillborn baby."

"My mother said it's a gentle heirloom that's supposed to help the family heal from their loss."

"Your mother is fucking mental."

I show myself to the front door, the rest of my evening passing in a blur of tears and uncertainty, like every day after that. I hide away in my home, sending Parker off and ignoring his calls whenever possible—anything to avoid the public and their rumors, suspicion, and lies. Police agree it's an awful coincidence that two of my partners and a baby have met a tragic end in such a short time, but apart from belated witness testimony, they can't prove a damn thing. You know what that makes me?

A dangerous woman.

Recovering from this loss is too much to handle. The death of my husband was bad enough, but I now believe the death of a child is not something you ever recover from. Parker is pretty much all I have left, and he sticks around the neighborhood for another month or two, but I think I've managed to finally push him away, too. I've ruined enough lives; there's no point in me corrupting his.

"I don't want you to stay here anymore, Parker," I tell him over dinner. I leave out the reason. He doesn't need to know it's because it's too hard having a living, breathing man—who happens to look a hell of a lot like my late husband—walking around my neighborhood and knocking on my door, dredging up the painful memory of Zayne's life.

The fact that my eyes are sealed shut when I say it is proof enough for him.

"I know you don't mean that. You need me."

He reaches out to grab my hand, but I pull it away so he can't touch me. He stares at me for a long time before speaking again. My eyes never leave the table.

"It hurts too much to see you like this, Clarisse. If it's that upsetting for you to have me here, I'll go." He pauses and tries to make eye contact with me, but I withdraw from the situation entirely.

He watches me leave the table and walk down the hall. I feel his eyes on me until we're separated by a wall. I rush into the bedroom and close the door between us. I stand there for the next five minutes, listening.

It doesn't take him long to collect his things. I hear him approach my bedroom door when he finishes. His knuckles knock against my door a few times to get my attention.

I stumble backwards and then freeze in place, holding my breath.

"When you're ready to talk, you know where to find me." I hear every step he takes toward the front door. It sounds so final, but not half as final as the sound of the door slamming shut behind him.

Parker's final words ring in my ears for days, interchanging with all the other demons haunting me. He's disappeared from my life—just like Zayne had. I've been suffering in the dark ever since.

Going against Parker, my doctor, and everyone else who gives a damn about me, I detain myself to my home, lock that mother-fucking door, and throw away the key. Months pass where I leave only to stock up on a few groceries at the market up the street, simply to sustain life, not enjoy it.

I wrap my jacket tightly around myself and wear Zayne's favorite ball cap to hide my eyes. Not only do I not want to face the locals, but I fear that someone is officially out to get me. I quickly walk up the street, my eye balls shooting from one parked car to the next. As soon as I can, I blend into the crowd and enter the market, finding the first food booth with fresh dairy and vegetables. I quickly grab a red pepper, a dozen eggs, and some apples. I'm convinced that someone's following me.

Before, I wasn't sure whether it was all in my head, but now I'm more than certain that someone is watching me. Eyes mark my every move and document my every purchase. I just know it. I'm being persecuted this very minute, and the only place I'm safe is inside the house that Zayne built. I pay the man at the cash register, forget about the rest of my little trip, and hightail it back to my house, carrying a single paper bag of produce.

One of my neighbors is standing in his front yard when I return home, but I keep my ball cap pulled low, and stare at the sidewalk. I hug the bag of groceries to my chest, and hide behind it. Still, he notices me.

"You should really think about mowing that lawn today."

I don't have time for chitchat. Whoever's following me might catch up and get me. I try to ignore the asshole talking and break into a light jog across my overgrown front lawn.

"That grass isn't going to cut itself, you know."

With my key clutched in my palm, I climb the stairs to my house and escape from the threat. So, the length of the grass pisses off the neighbors. I could care less. I bet it was an asshole like him who mowed over my husband and made me this way.

I let myself into the house and lock the door. I peer out the peephole, but no one's walking up my front sidewalk. I head to the kitchen and drop the paper bag onto my countertop, trying to focus on my happiest memories. Darkness consumes them all. Once I've got everything put away, I pace to my guest bedroom and take a handful of sleeping pills. I guzzle down the rest of my water and crash in my bed.

I am so over this day.

I'm not satisfied until a pillow is swallowing my head. If I could only stay that way forever. I open my eyes, feeling buried in this eternal hell. I wake, like I always do, at the crack of dawn in my guest bedroom. I really should quit calling it my guest bedroom, since I live here now.

Day after day, I wake and I crash. Wake and crash. Wake. Crash.

The next day is better than the last, the next day a little better, and the next even better yet. Eventually, I quit visiting the doctor for refills altogether and things become very clear again.

I don't know why today feels different, but it does. Instead of hovering restlessly in my living room, I turn on an old exercise show I used to stay fit with. It's amazing what a little sweat will do for a broken spirit. I fill a glass with tap water and swallow it back, staring at the dark drapes that protect me from the outside world. For the first time in the past year, I walk across the room with a purpose and pull on the long, white strings on the blinds. A blinding yellow light casts sunshine onto my creamy carpeted floor.

The moment of revelation steals the air from my lungs when I see I've missed one of the wedding photographs on the wall. I pace to the picture and scowl at the smiling woman, with both hands settling on my now bony hips. Somehow I'd managed to pull off *happy* with Zayne, even after all the trials I'd been put through.

I wonder if I'll ever be able to move my lips into a smile like that again. It doesn't hurt to try, but the muscles in my face refuse to turn my lips upwards. I back away from the picture and then violently pry the frame from the wall, taking a chunk of drywall with it. I turn over the frame and lower it onto the mantle, face down, with determination replacing the old tears in my eyes.

Suck it up, Clarisse. This is your life now. It's not going to get any better than this. You might as well drop the snivelling act.

I spin around and move into the hallway, being careful to avoid any other triggers. When I reach the end of the hall, I pull open both drapes at once with a harsh tug. Dust sprinkles over me like it's snowing, and it makes me sneeze. I glance into the backyard, but only for a second. When I see the small plastic baby swing toppled over in the overgrown grass, I nearly lose it.

I steal my eyes from the graphic images passing through my mind like a hideous home video and shake them from my head. My eyes zero in on the door I've left closed for the past year. I move to it without removing my eyes from the door handle and, with a swift twist, fling open the door to my master bedroom.

There, before me, are all of Zayne's things I couldn't bear to part with after he died. Everything had been tossed into the room in a haphazard heap of memories and things. Perhaps before I pushed Parker away, I could have gotten him to take all of Zayne's things with him. Now I have a huge, difficult task ahead of myself.

I will do it—I have to—but not today, and not all at once. Dragging my feet, I crack open a few more sets of curtains and then mope all the way over to my sofa. I don't miss the other wedding photograph on the mantle, or my very first ultrasound photo of my little peanut that is peeking out from a book on the tall wooden shelf.

And what about all those little things that were once hiding in the shadows? Like the nick in the paint, next to the light switch. To you, it means nothing. To me, that's where Zayne scratched the wall with the box for the new crib, because he wouldn't let his pregnant wife lift a finger. That damn thing took him hours to put together, because he insisted he was a handyman. I always laughed at him. A handyman? Maybe in another lifetime.

He can be so iron-willed sometimes.

See?

That.

No amount of paint will make me forget that Zayne was once here and now he's been robbed of life, just like my sweet baby boy.

In the dark, it is so much easier to avoid the little things like that, but there's no avoiding the constant flow of reminders of how alone I am in this world. Even when I brush my fucking teeth, I'm reminded of the way Zayne used to hug me from behind and reach for his toothbrush, because he was too impatient to wait for me to finish.

My heart aches with a hurt that shouldn't even exist, but I am lost without him. So much time has passed, and yet my life continues to be in ruins like the day he left me. I know why today is different. Today is the day everything changed for me. It's the anniversary of their deaths. Sweeping that reminder away, I scoop up my car keys and head outside.

I don't bother to look in the mirror or pull on a bra. I know I look like shit in my sweatpants and T-shirt. I know Zayne's car insurance isn't even valid, but I don't care. I need to get out.

The car groans to life after a couple of tries, and I drive around until the gas tank runs empty. I roll up to the gas station on fumes, but I make it there before the car stalls out. A young mechanic offers to pump my gas.

"Give it twenty," I say.

I remain in the car and stare into space while the boy smears dirty water over my windshield. As he wipes the window clean, a smiling blonde woman moves into my line of sight. I shake my head to see whether I'm actually seeing this correctly, but yes! It's her. It's really her—that selfish woman who's responsible for killing my husband!

At first, I tell myself it's just a sick, twisted trick I'm playing on myself. It's not really her. It can't possibly be; and yet I continue to watch her, like she's an actress in my favorite Netflix series. She's speaking to a gentleman in a suit, smiling widely at him before handing him a paper from the stack in her black leather folder. She shakes his hand and twirls away.

The second she disappears around the corner of the building, the man crumples the small paper into a ball and tosses it into the overflowing trash can next to him. I wait for him to go inside the gas station, and then frantically scramble out of my car and across the parking lot to hunt down that note. I retrieve the crumpled paper and stuff it in the pocket of my oversized pants, ignoring the boy calling out to me from the pump.

I consider chasing the woman down. I would love to run her over with my car. Wouldn't that be ironic? My lips curl upwards for the first time since Zayne and my baby passed. Crafting this woman's demise gives me great pleasure, and revenge would be so sweet. A light bulb moment has the smile quivering on my face. My lips don't know what's happening to them.

Hurrying back to my car, I reach into my purse and toss the pump attendant a twenty. The kid looks confused when the bill floats like a feather to the pavement because he's still pumping gas into my car's tank. His shock continues when I turn on the car and pull away, spilling gas all over his shoes.

I wave at him in my rear-view mirror and flatten the paper atop my lap, as I drive toward my house.

Congratulations, Marissa Meyers.

According to this invitation, the uppity bitch is up for a promotion. She has a party coming up next weekend at one of the most beautiful and sophisticated hotspots in New York.

Isn't her life just perfect?

This feels like a gift handed to me from the heavens. Who knew revenge could be delivered up to me in such a neat little package? I've heard that the door to that party room is always tighter than tight, but there has to be a way for me to get in.

My tires squeal as I turn into my driveway, my car screeching to a halt. I race into the house and find the cell phone that I had turned off for the better part of a year. First, I log in as a guest on the neighbor's unlocked Wi-Fi, and then I Google the event. Before long, I've scribbled down a list of the high-profile gentlemen attending. I'm sure one of them can use a piece of arm candy for the evening.

I open up the garage, pull out the riding lawn mower, and fire that bitch up. I pull down the lever that controls the blades, and step on the gas pedal. While I clean up my yard, I remember just how good I can look if I try. I know that if I keep exercising, put on a little weight, and maybe get a tan, I can pull off young and healthy. I've got two weeks to make it happen. My favorite part: they'll never see me coming.

Within an hour, my yard looks clean, and I'm scheduled for a waxing appointment. I admit I'm well overdue for a haircut. I take a quick shower and dress for the day. With towel-dried hair, I walk outside and down the sidewalk toward the nearest beauty salon. I'm a few steps away from my destination when I realize what I've just done. My feet become glued to the pavement. A wild, orange cat stares at me from its perch on the windowsill of the storefront, like I'm brainless.

This is the first time I've set foot on this sidewalk since the accident, and this cat seems to be the only one who cares. My eyes zero in on the spot up the road. A deep breath slows my racing heart.

You've come this far already.

Reminding myself of Marissa Meyers' smiling face, I push through the front doors of the salon and demand a makeover. They don't disappoint. Believe it or not, there's a pretty woman hiding behind all my overgrown hair and downturned lips. The woman at the salon with wild, purple hair and a contagious smile has the most fun, giving me a hairstyle that'll pull all my hard work together.

When I return to my house, I stop to have a look at myself in the front mirror. My eyes widen at the sight. I look like a frigging rock star. I flip my hair over my shoulder and try to smile, again. It hurts at first, but I feel my muscles responding to the new movement. My mouth is so shaky; it's ridiculous. I'll have to practice it some more if I plan to pull it out again any time soon.

By the time the night of the party arrives, I've nailed the city diva look with a seductive smile, glossy hair, and dark-painted eyes. I've snagged myself a wealthy, old man from the high-class pub up the road. He's agreed to take me out to an extravagant meal if I agree to attend an exclusive party—Marissa Meyers' promotion party—with him. No one knows about any ulterior motives spinning around in my head. They all believe I'm planning to take this old fart for everything he's worth, which is a given, but there are a handful of other gold diggers present with similar motives.

Old man Marshall escorts me to the snooty party and waves at a few guests who stare at his new arm candy. They have no clue what I'm really up to. Neither does Marshall. I don't expect he will even notice when I survey the room, but my senses are unpracticed, and I underestimate how many eyes are on me.

"Looking for someone, Clarita?"

I turn to face him and smooth my fingers over his tie, flattening it against his rounded body. "What are you talking about?" I slap at him playfully. "I don't know another soul here. Only you, Marshall."

He clearly likes it that way. He's proud to have me on his arm, a good thirty years his junior.

"Why don't we try to fix that?" He offers me his elbow and I take it, following him dutifully to a crowd of slightly younger men with stick-thin models on their arms.

"Jasper Nix, please meet Clarita Black."

I accept the gentleman's hand and allow him to kiss mine.

"Oh," I say as if this pleasantly shocks me, while the woman next to Mr. Nix stirs with jealousy. I smile at the poor thing.

You can have him.

Marshall continues with the introductions. The more fake smiles and superficial introductions I survive, the closer I get to the bottom of my rainbow. Marissa Meyers is now close enough that I can almost stretch my arms out and strangle her with my bare hands. I see how happy the bitch is. She doesn't deserve it. It's as if nothing's happened to her. Her life is the same as it was one year ago. Wait, no. She appears to be doing better now than she was a year ago. It's like she's forgotten entirely about what she's done. That changes today.

Time to make her remember.

My eyes light up when I see her move toward the restroom. Now's my chance to approach her. I smile at my wealthy sponsor and smooth my hand up and down his arm before turning to the group of fuddy-duddy businessmen. "Please excuse me." I pat Marshall's chest, knowing no one expects anything more of me than to stand around and look pretty. "I'll be right back."

"Don't keep me waiting."

I flash a seductive glance back at him, that has all the men mumbling, and then I refocus on the reason for my escape. I stalk across the floor in four inch heels, drawing every man's eye within a twenty foot radius. Following this woman's daily life has become a sick ritual that I obsess over every waking minute. My limbs tremble with excitement now that I get to make my first contact.

I follow her into the women's restroom and check over my shoulder to make sure no one is behind me. The lock slides quietly into place, until a woman approaches me from the sinks.

"Wait for me," she cheers, hurrying to the door.

I suck in a breath, let the woman out of the room with a practiced smile, and then relock the door. When I peer around the corner, she's there—*the bitch who ruined my life.*

I try to find something wrong with this woman, but everything appears to be so picture-perfect for her. Her face is flawless, not a hair misplaced on her head, and her dress is obviously the result of a well-paid tailor. The skirt cuts off just below her knees and fits her like a glove. I wonder how she even walks in those tall, skinny heels.

Our eyes finally meet in the mirror, of all places. I'm applying another coat of my ruby red lipstick. She surely doesn't recognize me as the woman whose married life she ended.

"I like your shoes," I say, wishing I could think of something more clever to say after all this time.

"Thanks," she replies with a smile. She glances at my shoes, looking for a compliment to repay me, but hesitates.

Bitch.

"Who's that guy you're here with?" I ask, hoping maybe that will be the spark to jumpstart the conversation. Her husband is a good-looking man, clearly successful, and unmistakably younger than her.

"Who, Jase? Oh, he's my husband. A waste of space, if you ask me, but that doesn't leave this room," she adds, smirking.

Bam. That's the statement I needed to hear in order to set this friendship off on the right foot.

"It can't be all that bad," I say.

As I listen to the woman's rendition of her horrible life, I realize the pretty picture she paints for the public is far from the truth. I save my smile and nod to acknowledge what she's saying, even if I don't agree with her self-centered issues and superficial troubles.

"Hey, at least he tends to the kids," she says, making it so much easier for me to do this to her.

When we move to exit the restroom, I delicately unlock the door and act shocked to see a line of ladies outside of it. I shrug my shoulders at Marissa and return to the party with her. Her husband snares my gaze from afar. He smiles that charming smile and walks toward us.

"Who is this beauty you've been hiding from me, Marissa?"

He takes my hand and sinks into my eyes. He obviously doesn't recognize me, either. Had neither of them picked up a newspaper after the accident? Our faces were plastered all over it for weeks.

I smile back at him, thinking dirty thoughts about how I'm going to rip these two apart for good. I can't wait to make a public spectacle of them.

"Oh, you know what? How rude of me! I didn't even ask your name," Marissa chimes, using drama to tear her husband's eyes from mine.

"Clarrr—rita. Clarita," I say, nearly blowing my cover for the second time tonight.

Jase shakes my hand. "Well, Clarrr-rita," he says, emphasizing my name. "I hope to see you again sometime real soon."

"Yes. Absolutely," I say, admiring the way he admits his

attraction to me in front of his wife.

"I'm Marissa," his wife adds, slipping in between us. "But I'm sure you already knew that."

Her high-pitched laugh gives me goosebumps, and I just barely shed my scowl in time to return a smile as Marshall scoops me away for the rest of the evening.

23: My Best Shot

The night couldn't have gone any better. My revenge will be sweet. Marissa Meyers' secret life will soon become a public exhibition. After meeting Jase, I realize I might even enjoy this. A total waste? We'll see about that. He puts a handsome smile on for the socialites, but I doubt they know all the names his wife calls him behind closed doors. They will soon.

First, I have to figure out whether he's sticking around for the money, or if he's keeping it together for their kids—an honorable thing to do, I suppose. I have different plans for him. Frankly, nothing else matters. I only get this one shot to destroy this woman's life, and I'm going to make for damn sure that I get it right.

A few days later, wearing skinny jeans and heels, with a loose-fitted grey tank top and a black bandeau, I attack my unavailable man. Why am I doing this? His wife deserves to live the hell that I'm living—to see what's it's like to be me.

This is going to be a cake walk. Jase frequents the park a few blocks away from where I live. He's watching his kids, so I keep it short and innocent. I cross the deep green grass and rest against the bench he's sitting on. I stop just long enough for small talk, seeing that he's overtired.

"Hey, you. Long day?"

He sighs, glancing up at me. He does a double take before recognizing me from the other night. "You have no idea."

I smile. "Why don't you tell me?"

That gets his attention, causing him to stand up, but he doesn't spill all the beans at once. With his hands tucked in his pockets, I quickly learn that I'm going to have to earn his trust before he opens himself up more to me.

A few days later, I run into him again, not so accidentally, at a small restaurant I know he likes to visit at this time of day.

"Hey," I say when he walks up behind me. "Funny seeing

you here." It's only my third visit to the cash register this morning, but of course he doesn't know that.

"Let me get that for you." He pays for my coffee and we leave together.

I give him a few minutes of small talk and he ushers me away from the foot traffic, telling me about the private, but dirty, court battle with his wife.

"You can't tell anyone this. I'm trusting you, Clarita."

Trust is such a fragile thing. He would be wise not to trust anyone—especially not me.

"I know I can't keep up like this for much longer. There's only so much a guy can take."

Big surprise—the witch is trying to flush him down the toilet. It's no wonder her attitude has been grating on his nerves. I can't believe he's agreed to stay in the house and act like nothing's wrong for publicity's sake.

"You're a good man," I say.

Jase huffs. "It's all for my boys. Marissa can go fuck herself."

I laugh softly, and the sound is magnificent, but I quickly hide my joy when I notice how all this lying to his kids has been piling up on his conscience. It looks like he can use some relief. I happen to specialize in that department.

Jase takes a sip from his coffee and sighs. "I quit my job and gave up everything for her. I left my family behind to start a new life with her here in the city. She went out and found a new group of friends, but to be honest I have none."

"You have me," I say, catching on to his hand and connecting with his eyes.

For a second, my own conscience threatens to test my nerve, but then Jase sighs again and turns the problems back on himself.

"I'm sorry. I'm sure listening to my boring life is the last thing a beauty like you wants to do with her day."

"You stop it. You're fine." I release his hand before it gets awkward. Playing hard to get has never felt this fulfilling.

"What do you say I make it up to you?" he asks.

That's what I'm talking about!

But before he can spit it out, I say, "Another time? I have to run."

I make a mad dash for the sidewalk, very pleased with today's progress, even if being hit with a dose of reality doesn't feel nice at all. It won't be long now. The stage is set. I thought it'd take more time to earn his trust, but I think I've got this one in the bag.

I leave Jase alone for a few days, knowing I'll stay fresh on his mind the entire time, but this alone-time is dangerous. It gives me too much time to curl up in a ball, get all red-faced, and fret. On day three, I'm all worried-out and a little too stir-crazy to wait any longer. This will work. It has to.

If I can't be happy, no one can.

Heading off on foot, I pop in a piece of cool mint gum and sling my purse across my chest. I know exactly where I'm heading. I plan to strike where Jase is at his weakest—while he's at the playground with his sons. It's my best shot

24: Revenge is Sweet

The sun is hot, and the excitement coursing through me doesn't make the heat any more bearable. The sound of whiny kids is music to my ears when I start down the winding path toward the kiddy equipment. Sure enough, Jase is there—just as scheduled.

I zero in on my target and make a beeline for him, holding my sandals in my right hand. The long grass whispers across my toes. The breeze flips my hair back, exposing rosy cheeks. I can't wipe the undeniably pleasant smile from my face. No one can spoil this moment for me.

Look at him! I still can't believe he's a house-husband; it's obvious it's not by choice. To the unsuspecting passersby, Jase looks like an intelligent, well-mannered businessman, raising his children on his own. It's unfortunate that I have to destroy his life completely and make that a reality. The poor thing is wasted, anyways. I believe his wife called him a *waste of space*. The only thing I see is a man wasting away due to lack of use.

A good, strong man like that could always use a little extracurricular activity in his life, and I doubt he's getting any from his perfect little soon-to-be ex-wife.

I approach him with determination in my step, ready to make my move. I know I have psychological issues—that doing this to him isn't quite right—but I refuse to be the only one who suffers here. I am going to take what I can get and ruin this family in the process. I slide up next to where Jase has just barely settled. When he smiles, I know he isn't totally lost. It looks like he hasn't done that in a long time, though.

"Smiling shouldn't be a hidden talent for you," I say.

His eyes meet mine. "I could say the same to you."

I hide my fear—the fear that he sees right through me—with facts. The fact is he has two things I don't: money and family. From what I hear, any combination of those two things tends to make people happy. Having barely scraped by on my own two feet for the better part of my life, I don't have enough experience in the matter to fully comprehend this guy's problems, but I'd be willing to bet it's all his wife's fault.

I take the seat next to him on the blue aluminum bench. I know it's a dumb question, because I know the answer, but I ask anyway. "Come here often?" The change of conversation works like a charm.

He smiles again. "Every Tuesday and Thursday." He glances at the group of kids playing in the mulch. "Right on schedule." He sighs, admitting his defeat.

I check on the mother forming the other half of his playdate and then smile. She's clearly more concerned about her own child, swatting his grubby hands and wiping his snot nose, than paying attention to me with Jase. She doesn't even notice me sitting here with him, which is exactly what I bank on. I glance back at the kids.

"Which ones are yours?"

Jase turns to me and smiles—but not the tired smile he'd just given me, rather a devious one, like the one he'd served up at his wife's party. "Let's be honest here for a second. You don't care about nap times, and you don't care about my kids."

I don't know where he's going with this, but I've got nothing against being honest when it furthers my position. "Okay. Let's say that's true."

His smile widens, and I like what it does to me. "I don't do this often," he says.

I bite my bottom lip to keep from smiling too hard.

He hunches forward, resting his forearms on his thighs. "Okay, I've never done this before. But I have to say it. You intrigue me."

He tilts his head up to look at me and smiles. I can't tell whether it's in a feisty way, or if he's only squinting because the sun is really bright. Regardless, he raises his eyebrows and holds them there, the sun kissing his skin in places I intend to get familiar with very soon.

"*I* intrigue *you*?" I ask.

"Are you saying the feeling is mutual?"

I love playing hard to get, but I'm ready to get while the getting is good. With a feminine shrug, I casually reach out and flick a lock of blond hair from his eyes.

"You're a very handsome man—obviously undervalued. Your wife doesn't deserve you."

He sighs, smiling at the ground between his legs, and then glances up at me again. I lay my arm on the bench behind him and, when he sits all the way up, I play with the hair at the base of his neck. He doesn't ask me to stop. A ripple of power passes through me. I can see he's enjoying the attention. I give him a little more before standing to my feet to leave.

"I have to get going, but it was nice talking to you, Jase." I grab my sandals and walk away. I have to go because I want very much to take him home with me, but I know now is not the time and this is not the place after all. There's the other half of his play date, and then there's the kids.

I guess I haven't thought it all through.

Still, this could be my only chance. I need him to know that I'm not just playing. I want him. So with a provocative smile, I turn back. "Same time tomorrow?"

"Thursday," he admits. "I actually have tomorrow off. The kids go to work with Marissa on Wednesdays."

I smile pointedly. "Tomorrow it is."

By noon the next day, we're crashing into his front foyer and fighting with each other's clothes, because we can't get them off fast enough. One second, he's rolling on a condom, and the next he's lifting me onto his lap and thrusting into me like a deprived sailor.

I'm not going to lie. It feels good. Okay, fine, it's really fucking fantastic. Not only does this man have years of experience in the bedroom, but the mistress aspect makes it that much more mysterious and hot. For me, the fact that his wife has no idea ups the ante to an undeniably pleasant point. He gets me off, helps me pull myself back together, and lets me out the back door, kissing me like he means it.

I walk home with a smile on my face, wondering when I'll see him again.

At first, I believe my revenge will cure me, but it only feeds my illness. I grow hungry for artificial love, lust—call it what you will. It keeps me alive. But after a few weeks, our violent quickies turn into a regular routine, and an all too familiar ache lodges in my chest. My fun has run its course.

"Put a little effort into this, Clarisse. Will you, please?" Jase begs, knowing my mind is elsewhere.

It truly is a shame that our little arrangement has to end so soon. Jase is a total dime, with the most attractive blond happy trail. I continue to bounce on top of his dick, but it's half-hearted and we both know it.

He pushes me aside. "What's your problem today?"

I think to keep quiet but decide that I've had enough of this already. "I'm trying to think of something to say that doesn't start with *fuck you.*"

He glares at me, and it's as intense as his raging hard on. Then I hear a door click shut downstairs. He doesn't seem to notice, because he's standing there very naked with me is his marital bedroom. He makes no move to cover himself or to shoo me into hiding. He's too caught up with my sudden attitude change to detect anything else.

"You don't mean that," he states.

"Not sorry," I admit, and I kind of mean it. But, instead of pulling out my phone and snapping a video of Marissa's fully erect husband walking toward me like I'd planned to, I decide to bend over the bed and steal Jase's complete attention with the curve of my ass.

"Are you coming over here to punish me?—to show me how bad of a girl I'm being today?"

He laughs and playfully slaps my ass as soon as he can reach it.

I know he wants to.

"Harder," I beg, knowing it will turn him on even more.

I'm not the least bit surprised when I hear the slap of his hand on my soft skin. Once. Twice. Three times. He spanks my ass so hard the sound surely carries down the hall, and it turns me on so much I moan, because I know this is it—the moment I've been waiting for.

Jase climbs between my spread legs, massages my tender skin, and grabs a hold of my scarred hips. This next bit is the best kind of shocking. He fucks me. With his pelvis slapping against my upturned ass, and me moaning with undeniably the best pleasure of my life, he fucks me. That's right about when his wife enters the room. I see her out of the corner of my eye, but act like I don't, making her witness the way her husband's dick takes my orgasm.

I scream as Jase comes hard, and continues to pump into me, before noticing our little visitor at the door. He's so caught up in the moment that he doesn't even pull out when he turns to face his wife. I smile as he pulses inside me and then slowly eases out.

See, Marissa? It still works. If you don't put it to good use, someone else will.

I roll aside, finally acknowledging the woman in the room. The fact that she has yet to say anything tells me she enjoys watching.

"I should go." I quickly yank on my underwear and pull my dress over my head, rather giddy with how this turned out. I carefully hide my smile.

"What the fuck is going on here?" she finally asks her husband with a dramatic whisper.

As I pass the bitch, she finally recognizes me. "You!"

Of course she'd recognize me now, with my hair a wild mess, the mascara smeared under my eyes, and the straight face I stick her with. "Yeah. I'm the one who you widowed, bitch."

I wait for her reaction to my select words, but she has no idea what I'm talking about—not a fucking clue. It's clear to me now that she only recognizes me from her snooty little party. My anger fuels the fire raging in my heart.

"Clarita?"

"Clarisse Blackwell." I reach my hand out for a shake, knowing she won't take it. "Does that name ring a bell? How about Zayne Varela? Maybe that will *jog* a few memories." I steal my hand back as my face turns into a dark scowl. "It should. You murdered my husband, you dumb bitch." I glance back at Jase. "See you around."

25: Clean House

Rumors of the Black Widow striking again fill the streets. Weeks of tactless maneuvers to comfort myself only drive me deeper into a depression that threatens to consume me. To ease the pain, I cause pain to others—make them see how it feels to be me.

Nice, huh?

I recognize who I have become while staring at myself in the mirror. It's time to go. I need to get out of New York City, away from all the finger pointers and name callers. I need to find a new place to call home and create a new identity for myself, just like I did when I came to this godforsaken place. There's nothing left for me in Forest Hills.

I sell what furniture I can for cash and leave Zayne's car behind, since I can't afford the payments anymore. I leave his overdrawn bank account, pack my bags, and abandon our beautiful house. Receiving the foreclosure notice from the bank speeds up my plans, and I'm shacked up in a cheap motel with a one-way ticket to the other end of the country before the last of my insurance proceeds even reaches my wallet.

The bus ride to San Francisco is a long one—seventy-five hours in all, with thirty-one unique stops and five transfers—but the price is right, and it is all I can afford on my limited budget. I ignore the bumps in the road and the dude decked out in a weathered jean jacket and pony tail. Instead of making a new friend or two, I mind my own business and stare out my window.

I plug my ears with music and sink into my thoughts. I need a plan and a good one. What the hell am I going to do with myself now? I thought that two wrongs would make a right, but I don't feel right. On the final leg of my trip, I close my eyes to fend off the dizziness, pop a sleeping pill, and slip under. I don't awaken until I'm tapped on the shoulder by the homeless drifter sitting next to me.

"Is this you?" She points a finger across the bus.

My eyes flutter forward where I see my destination printed clearly across the building we're parked to. "Oh! Thank you."

"A safe trip to you, my dear," she shouts after me as I hustle up to the crowd of others already exiting the bus.

Carrying all of the belongings to my name strapped over my shoulder in an oversized backpack, I arrive at my new home on foot: a filthy motel room with a name as raunchy as the room itself. With a key dangling from the greasy silver doorknob, I scrunch my nose, and let myself in the retched place. I kick the door shut and drop my bag on the few feet of ceramic tiles at the door, noticing the way everything is covered in a ground-in layer of dirt. It's pretty sad that the dirty grey tiles are the cleanest spot in the place.

I assess the beige carpet that can be best described as filthy. I feel dirty just standing on it, and I'm wearing shoes. Years of wear and tear show from the quantity of rips and stains on the brown-plaid furniture. Deplorable things have gone down in this room. The smell is strong enough to gag a maggot. I try to avoid what I'll call a *coffee stain* in the middle of the room; the truth is, I fear it's not coffee at all.

I feel like I've walked into an undiscovered crime scene.

Knowing I won't last in here very long, I dig through my bag for some clean clothes. Even though I'm not feeling very cheeky, I go for a mini skirt that makes me look younger than I am and pair it with a fashionable shirt. As I pull off my socks and step right into my one-and-only pair of strappy sandals, an unrecognizable scratching noise on the floor makes me freeze in place.

Oh shit. Something is under the bed.

It smells like someone has hidden a dead body under there, after defecating in the bathtub. I don't want to do it, but not knowing is worse. I cross the room toward the dingy queen-sized bed, cautiously getting to my knees and reaching for the sheet. I lift the stale bed covering hesitantly, leaning closer to the stench to get a better look.

There's a single stream of light that hits a very small area of the floor under the bed. The rest of the space is flooded by darkness.

I squint into the shadows under the bed and find my worst nightmare hiding there—Finlay's angry face staring back at me.

I tell myself no—it's not possible!—but he looks so real. My wide eyes burn, but I can't blink. I remind myself to breathe, but I can't do that either.

"Is this real?" I whisper with the last of my breath.

Finlay's face moves quickly toward me and I scream, banging my head on the bed frame and falling backwards onto my ass. I notice something skittering across the floor and fumble, like a crab walking backwards, to get away from the critter. It's a mouse—only a fucking mouse.

My first breath is a gasp that doesn't quite reach my lungs. I slam my fisted hand against my chest three times before a cough leaves my mouth. What starts out as a cough, turns into a gag, and I know if I don't get out of here soon, I'm going to leave another stain on the floor. I kick my bag as I pass it, and it hits the wall near the door. Why didn't I splurge for the slightly nicer, if only clean, motel across the street? Oh yeah, because I'm nearly broke.

As I yank open the door, a piece of paper floats to the floor like a feather falling from the sky. It lands in a stream of late afternoon sunshine peeking through the thick, grey clouds, like a signal that encourages me to scoop it up. I bend over and read the large printed letters: MYSTERY TOUR. The date on the mini-flyer says it's tonight. I pick it up and flip it over, but there's no further information on the back.

I slap it across my other hand a few times, debating whether I'm ready to go out in public again so soon. This paper didn't just magically land there; someone put it there. I look one way and then the other. There's a woman dressed like a hooker entering a room a few doors down from mine, but other than that I seem to be alone.

I glance back into my new home and make a quick

decision, slamming the door between us. I can't go back in there, where I'll surely drive myself insane. This tour sounds like exactly what I need to reinvent myself. I don't care how I've come to learn about it. I need the breather. It will be good for me.

With a smile, I fold the page up, stuff it in my purse, and walk up the street to the nearest diner to kill some time and grab a quick bite to eat. When I settle into a shit brown booth seat, I pull out my old cell phone and check the message using the free Wi-Fi. Fucking lawyers. Apparently they can't wire my insurance proceeds to me because my claim is being audited. Fucking ridiculous, is what it is. So much for dinner.

I consider leaving, but I've already come this far. I'll have to settle for a coffee. With thirty-two dollars left in my wallet, I dial a local cab company.

A ditsy waitress sidles up next to me, ignoring my unavailability. She cocks her hip out and props her hand prominently atop it. "You can't sit here."

I glance around the room. She can't possibly be talking to me. There are three similar tables in our immediate vicinity, and they're all vacant. "Like fuck I can't," I answer her, just as the cab company answers my call.

"This table is reserved. See the sign?" She picks up one of the rectangular cards from the table next to mine and drops it on my table. "*Reserved.*"

I hear a foreign man shouting questions in my ear.

"Can you excuse me for one minute, please?" I say into the phone as I place it face down on the table. I pick up the card she's just dropped there and show it to her. "Oh, you mean this card?" Then I fling it across the room. It conveniently lands on another table, which happens to be empty. "There. Problem solved."

I smirk as she stomps off and returns with another card. "You have to move. You can't sit here," she squawks, just as a young gentleman walks up behind her.

She spins around to greet him, smartening up her tone. "Oh! Mr. Decker, I'm so sorry about the inconvenience. I'm just trying to get this..." She pauses for dramatic effect. "...w*oman* to move."

I have a few names I'd like to call her, too. I step out of the booth but not to leave. The guy can see this confrontation is only turning hotter and steps in between us, smiling at the witch before turning to face me.

"Are you here alone?"

I look around. What does it look like? I nod without breathing a word to him.

"Mind if I join you?"

A smile breaks out on my face. I can't even hide it. I nod my head again, and he wastes no time sliding up next to me when I retake my seat in the booth. He then drapes his arm around the back of the bench and waits a few seconds for the waitress to pick her jaw up off the floor.

"I don't suppose you've taken Miss..."

"Blackwell," I add.

"Miss Blackwell's order, have you?" he asks her.

"Well, no," she answers sheepishly.

"What are you getting?" he asks me, gazing intently into my eyes. When I hesitate, he adds, "It's on me."

"Oh, in that case." I whip open the menu.

He chuckles as I order a number of things. I am absolutely starving. My stomach has been grumbling for at least three hours now, and I don't think I've eaten more than a couple of grapes I scammed off an old lady today on the bus, and a kid's slobbered-on penguin cracker.

The waitress continues to stare at us, waiting for who knows what.

"Run along," Decker tells her, shooing her with a couple flicks of his wrist. "We'll need a minute."

"Oh shit!" I pick up my phone and answer it. "Hello? Hello?" But no one's there. It's no surprise the taxi company hung up on me.

Decker looks curious. "Who were you calling?"

"A cab?" I don't even know why I pose it as a question— probably because Decker makes me feel surprisingly welcome in a very unwelcoming neighborhood.

"Where are you heading?"

I think twice before giving up any more information to him. I've already said too much. "Well, I, uh—"

"I'm happy to give you a ride. I have a stop to make, but my driver will take you anywhere within the city limits after that. What did you say your name was again?"

"It's Clarisse."

"Well, Clarisse, if you're worried that I might be a convict, don't. Every person in this city knows who I am. In fact, I would bet on it that you're the only one here who doesn't."

Although intrigued, I leave it alone and take his word for it. "Okay." I rummage through my purse, pull out the crumpled paper, and flatten it on the table. I point at the address of the starting point for the Mystery Tour but get distracted by the smile that has spread across his face. "What?"

"You," he says. "You're so cute."

I squint at him like he has me confused with someone else. "I know you aren't talking about me right now, so why don't you come out with it."

He leans closer, so the customers a few tables away can't hear him. "You actually expect me to believe that we're meeting here on accident."

"Um, yeah?" I honestly have no clue who this guy is and, frankly, I don't care.

"Huh." He sighs, wearing an attractive smile while watching me carefully. It looks like he's leaning more toward believing me. "You really have no idea who I am?"

"I really don't. And no offense, but it's not all that important to me."

"Wow. You are a piece of work. But I like you. Care to be my date tonight? Turns out, we have a lot in common."

I pick up the scrap of paper to remind him that I have plans. "I already told you, I'm going to this—"

Decker stops me in a heartbeat.

"I happen to be going to the same event. We might as well go together. It'll save you the cab fare, and I might even buy you a couple of drinks, if you play nice and smile for the cameras."

26: Change is Good

I settle into a smile. Decker is just begging me to ask who he is. I roll my eyes, but I won't be giving in that easily. Not knowing is more fun. He seems like a pretty nice guy—average-looking. He actually reminds me a little bit of Zayne, just chunkier around the middle. I enjoy pretending just for one second that my life hasn't been ripped out from underneath me. Glimmers of my old life—a happy one with Zayne—blur into reality.

Decker senses my distress and grabs for my hand, just as a handful of goons with cameras swarm us and start asking dumb questions.

"Come on. Let's ditch this joint," he says.

I collect my phone and purse, and he pulls me for the door so fast that I don't even know what's going on. "But—" I stretch my hand out toward the plate heading for our table, like it's my long lost lover.

"Put it on my tab," he tells the girl at the register while I snatch a fry off some guy's plate near the exit.

Decker smirks at me while he taps something into his phone with his free hand. "We're going to have a killer night."

I don't doubt it when he pulls me to the door of the long, black hummer that has just pulled up to the curb. A gentleman in a suit strides around the front of the sexy machine and opens the door for me. This all seems a little too good to be true. When I'd fallen backwards in my dirty motel room, had I bumped my head, and this is the result of too many gaseous fumes?

I don't know.

"Just get in," Decker says.

So I do.

The instant the black door closes behind me, a splash of liquor lines a glass and is glued in my hand for the next three hours. I've never had the luxury of drinking in a vehicle before, but I think I like it. There's a platter of fruit that I devour before realizing they must be liquor soaked, too.

The conversation is light and flows easier as the night rolls on. We have an amazing dinner in a private location that makes me happy to have agreed to leave the diner with him. After a long walk on a beach and a short nap on Decker's shoulder, he wakes me.

"Oh, shit. Did I fall asleep?" I ask him, fixing his rumpled jacket.

He smiles softly and moves my hair away from my face. "Don't worry about it. It's been a long night. I can take you back to your place, if you want."

"What? No. I still want to go out. I mean, unless you have plans that don't include me."

He looks at me for a long time. He's trying to read me but is failing miserably at it. "How do you do that? One minute you're sassy and arrogant, the next you're humble and unassuming. You're a beautiful mystery to me, Clarisse."

And I'd like to keep it that way.

He's staring into my eyes, waiting for me to give him something. The glassy look I find there tells me he's been juicing it the entire time I was asleep.

"So, what's your story?" Decker asks me suddenly, holding a strawberry out to me.

I take the fruit from his hand and rub the strawberry over his lips before giving him the first bite.

"Can't a girl have her secrets?"

He smirks and settles back into his seat, knowing I won't be divulging any more information about myself. "Fair enough."

It is then when I realize he is trying to get to know me better, and I don't even know his first name. "But, if we're going to be friends, maybe I should know what to call you." I play with his jacket some more. "I could stick with Decker, but something tells me that's not your favorite." I reach for more fruit. "What should I call you?"

"How about King? Yeah, I like that." He pours me a cool

glass of wine.

I snort when I laugh, and it makes him laugh, too. "Just tell me your name already."

His smile is handsome and confident. "Devlin Decker, but you can call me Dev."

The name doesn't ring a bell, but I agree to the shortened name because it really suits him. "Dev. I like it."

I take the crystal goblet from his hand and sip the wine, sinking back into an alcohol-induced trance. The night goes on, and I almost forget that there was somewhere we were supposed to be. Dev laughs at me a lot. I don't really think I'm saying anything particularly funny, and his laugh is different than Zayne's, but I'm happy to have a sidekick for the night. The free food and drink doesn't hurt.

By midnight, we're catching up with the last of the Mystery Tour at The Fox Shoppe, an adult entertainment hotspot. Dev holds me tight to his side from the second we leave the Hummer until we're inside the upscale nudie bar. Within minutes, Dev gets swamped by a pack of naked ladies and a few fully clothed ones. I'm left to tend to my fruity cocktail in peace at the bar.

"The mayor's son?" a minimally dressed bartender asks me while I suck on the cherry from my drink.

"I'm sorry?" I'm mostly concerned about the drink in my hand and don't even make eye contact with the woman.

"Devlin Decker. How did you land a date with the guy? He's like the number one bachelor in the city, and you're the new girl linking arms with him. Good for you! But I have to know. How'd you do it?"

When I start to talk about how I met Devlin, and look over to where he is standing, I notice how he's suddenly watching me from across the room. Within five seconds, he's lifting me from my seat and hooking on to my arm.

"Hey, Clarisse. You're coming with me." He grabs my hand and drags me toward the stage.

I'm too drunk to put up a meaningful fight.

"I see you're talking about me," he says menacingly.

"Actually, I didn't get a chance to, Mr. Mayor."

"Oh, shit. You figured it out, huh? I suppose that's why you're hiding away from me."

"I wasn't hiding."

"Oh, really? That's what it looked like to me."

"I'm not hiding," I repeat, growing anxious about the idea of him looking me up online.

His eyes flash up at a dancer who has come to pry a few dollars from his hand. He watches her do her thing and tucks a few folded bills under the band of her thong when she squats in front of him. Even with her ass in his face, Dev turns to me wearing a devilish smirk. "You should get up there."

"Yeah, no," I tell him, even though the faces on those bills he just gave that woman are still flashing like dollar signs in the back of my head.

"I'm sure you can dance way sexier than those bitches up there. It'll be fun," he insists.

I sit there and think about it. I could use a couple of dollars to my name, and I suppose it wouldn't kill me. "You just want to see me shake my ass."

"Yes," he agrees.

"But those women get paid to be up there."

"Are you kidding? It's amateur night. Can't you tell?" He helps me to my feet and waves at a bulky guy monitoring the stage. The man slowly walks toward me. He looks like trouble, but hey, I didn't do anything wrong!

Devlin pushes me toward the stage.

"Decker, no!" I warn him, polishing off my drink and placing the empty cup on the table.

He's still laughing when he hands me off to the big man wearing all black. "Show me what you're made of!"

The security guard takes my hand and helps me onto the stage. I look at the dude for a long moment, listening to the change in music. He nods at me, like a silent, *You can do it!*

Fuck it. What have I got to lose?

I bend forward, giving Decker an eyeful of cleavage. I point a drunken finger at him but forget what I was going to say. "I'll get you back for this."

The security guard feeds me the rules one at a time. ".. and most of all, have a good time."

I smile hesitantly.

He's amused by me, no doubt. "Did you hear a single word I just said?"

The wideness of my eyes is his answer.

Not a fucking word.

He laughs. "Dance a little. Take off your clothes, top layer only."

I nod, as it finally sinks in. They want me to take off my clothes.

"It'll drive the men wild," he growls in my ear, and then nudges me forward. "Go on. You're up."

Dance a little. Take my clothes off. Scatter when the song is over. I can do that.

I think.

I'm not exactly dressed for this, and I can't even remember what panties I'm wearing. *Oh, shit!* I turn back to the security guy and cup my hands around his ear. "My thong is see-through. Is that okay?"

It makes him smile, really big. He looks me up and down. "I'm sure it won't be a problem."

Devlin whistles like a construction worker and then outright laughs at me. I shoot him the finger and take the center stage. Of all the men watching me, I notice one in particular. He's sitting at the back of the room by himself. He's built the way I like, but glances downwards whenever I look in his direction, hiding beneath the peak of his ball cap. The way his shirt tugs across his chest is unmistakably attractive. Damn, but he looks familiar.

Could it be Parker?

All the lights twist around and land on me, blinding any chance at recognizing that face. The DJ approaches me and shoves a microphone in front of my mouth.

"What's your name and where you from?"

Instead of stating, *none of your god-damned business—* "The Black Widow," I answer. "I don't stay anywhere very long."

"Ooh. Okay," the DJ says, playing along.

But who am I kidding? I'm not playing. It's true. Whenever I get comfortable, shit slows down, right before it blows up in my face. For tonight, I'm going to play the girl these gentlemen want to take home, and that will have to be enough.

The DJ shouts over a steady beat. "Give it up for the Black Widow!" He hustles back to his turntable and spins a new beat just for me. It's dark and twisted and perfect for seducing a crowd.

All eyes zero in on me, and a spotlight blackens the rest of the stage, showering me in a sparkling light. Even though there are two other girls on smaller pedestals working their amateur magic, it feels like I'm the only girl in the room. Ignoring the ditsy blonde girl across from me, I remind every man there how flexible a gymnast can be. I tease them with the flip of my hair and an innocent dance, and then I surprise them all when I kick my right leg over my head, slowly easing it up the length of the silver pole. It's all in the tease, and I have that down to an art.

I twist my waist, drop to the floor, and lock my knees straight, giving a few select men a perfect view beneath my skirt. When the first guy tucks a twenty dollar bill into my waistband, I think I'm dreaming. I casually seek out Devlin in the crowd. He winks at me and then turns away, giving the other men a front row seat. I feel even more daring without his knowing eyes watching me.

I slowly peel off my shirt and spin around before dropping to my knees to crawl across the stage like an animal. More men approach the stage and try to give me their money.

Well, damn.

This is just unbelievable to me. All I'm doing is dancing to the song. It's even fun, and these men are practically throwing their money at me. I wonder what will happen when I strip right down to my skivvies. With the song practically over, I roll my hips, close my eyes, and slide my skirt down to my ankles. By the time it reaches the floor, there's a pile of bills forming there.

A cluster of men crowd me at the edge of the dance floor. The closer I get to them, the nearer the security gets. I flash the one who helped me onto the stage a coy smile that gets the attention of every last man staring at me. I crouch down and lean forward to allow a few fat fingers to tuck a bigger bill into the lacy strip of fabric across my hip. One of the younger men cops a little feel before being attacked by a security guard, but even that electrifies me.

I feel so powerful.

The applause when I leave the stage is just as electric. I'm alive with energy, my body fueled by adrenaline. I'm feeling really good about myself when Devlin grabs on to my waist and lowers me to the floor. As I pull on my clothes, security guard number one blocks me from being attacked by a mob of horny men. Another security guard comes to calm down the unruly ones while Devlin unwrinkles a handful of my easily earned cash and hands it to me.

Once I'm fully clothed, Devlin pulls me away from the crowd and huddles me close. We keep walking until we lose all but one of my stalkers—the one wearing the ball cap.

Devlin stops and stares him down. "You got a problem? Move along." He has no idea who he's talking to.

But I do.

Parker lifts his chin so I can see him underneath that hat, and stares right at me before turning toward Devlin. "You'd better be careful with that one. The Black Widow kills off her prey. If you aren't careful, you'll be her next victim."

Devlin loops an arm around my waist and pulls me against his side. "Yeah, but damn. She's hot, right?"

I'm smiling when he does this. Does that make Parker angry? He disappears before I can ask him, but I hope so.

27: You're Hired

I smirk at Devlin as I straighten my skirt. "That was wicked fun. It's been a while since I've done anything that exhilarating." I can't stop smirking as Devlin continues to play the protector. It's cute and all, but we both know we'll only ever be friends.

"Time to bolt, woman. The men are starting to hover."

He takes my arm and leads me toward the exit of the Fox Shoppe, just in time for me to catch Parker ducking out the back entrance.

"Where do you want to go, now?" Devlin asks me.

Would that offer still be open if he knew I came to this city chasing after another man? What if he knew that other man was now following me? I go to pull Devlin toward the back entrance, but a big hand reaches out to stop me. Another security guard dressed in the same black getup refuses to let us leave.

"Hold up a minute," the man says with one finger held in the air and the other holding his ear piece firmly in place.

The familiar security guy from the stage appears next to me and clasps on to my arm.

"Whoa, wait up," Devlin shouts. "Not so fast!" When he starts to wobble on his own two feet, I realize he's just as inebriated as I am.

The big security dude growls in my ear. "You know I'm not going to hurt you, right?"

I turn to face him. He's very tall. I find myself nodding before I even process what he's said.

"Are you looking for a job? You're just what the boss is looking for. I can hook you up, if you're at all interested."

I happen to be without a job, although I don't really feel like *hooking up* with anyone at the moment. Even though the feeling in the pit of my stomach tells me to turn around and walk away, I can't turn down this opportunity. "Show me the way."

Devlin lets me go when I'm pulled away. "I've got to go Clarisse." He shouts. "Catch up with me later?"

"Yes, later." I wave as the burly bouncer leads me through the Fox Shoppe. He weaves through a number of tables before reaching a pair of young women. He stops me with a glance.

The owner is a woman? Interesting. She's blonde, too, and looks barely twenty-one from the back.

"What's your real name, chicka?" the woman asks her prospective dancer.

"Candice," the red-haired girl answers. "But everyone calls me Candy."

"Right."

"My mother was a Broadway dancer."

The girl's hillbilly accent has me stifling a smile. She looks quite sophisticated with a full head of luscious red hair and intelligent freckles scattered on her cheeks, but her accent takes her intelligence down a notch.

"Ah-ha. That explains it." The boss flips her icy-blonde hair over her shoulder. "And why should I hire *you*?"

"I'll bring the men back for more." Her confidence had even me believing her.

"Okay." The boss laughs, and that familiar sound strikes me in the gut. "Come on back on Monday morning, and we'll give you a chance to audition. What do you say to that?"

"Thank you so much. You won't regret this," Candy says before taking off in a fit of excitement.

"Savari, I have another pretty one for you," my guard says, making the woman turn to face me.

When I hear her name, I freeze. When our eyes connect, I realize this is really happening.

It really is her!

Savari instantly wraps her arms around my neck with a girlish shriek. "Girl, what the hell are you doing here?"

I smile when she doesn't let me go. "I could ask you the same thing."

"This is my place.' She releases me and leaves her hands in the air, like she still can't believe it herself.

"Yours? Like, you manage it?"

"No, mine, like I own it." Her spine stiffens while my eyes bulge out of my head. "What? It's a classy establishment—at least as classy as a strip joint can get. And I am a good girl. This is all good, clean money." She points at me like I might put up an argument, but it's hard to feel too intimidated by a woman with such fair skin and fine features.

Yes, she was good, but the fact that she had to state the cleanliness of her money tells me that it's not all rainbows and sunshine like it once was for her.

"Your daddy gave you the money to fund a strip club? Wow, how things have changed."

She shakes her head. "Nope. I told you, this is all me. I've been cut off. It's for the best, really." She growls at me. "We have so much catching up to do!"

I keep smiling at her. It's been too long, and little about her has changed. Her hair's a bit longer, her highlights a bit whiter, but overall she's matured very nicely.

Savari assesses me the same way I do her. "Come on." She hooks on to my arm, and yanks me toward a door that reads: *Employees only*. Her security guard follows after us, like a tanker just daring someone to approach us. Savari swings around and pats him on the chest.

"Thanks, Derek, but I can take it from here."

Derek listens well. He leaves Savari's side and returns to his post without any further need for direction. Savari leads me through a series of halls and punches a few numbers into a keypad to unlock a tall, black door. She opens it up and flicks the lights on. I walk through the doorway and stop just inside the room. This is her office. It's modest, but you don't have to tell me it's hers; I just know it.

I walk over to the dark wood bookshelf and pick up the small frame meticulously placed opposite a business diploma. In it is a picture of four girls dressed in crimson cheerleading uniforms. Savari and I are sandwiched in the middle of two other rookies. I smile, remembering that as the best year of my life—the period I now call *before Finlay*. Tears well in my eyes, but that's just the liquor talking.

"Remember that day?" Savari asks me. "I don't think I've ever had that much fun." She takes the frame from my hand and stares at it, before returning it exactly where I'd lifted it from.

Sadness consumes me, as I remember how quickly my life had changed after that; I've become good at hiding my emotions over the years, and don't even need to clear my throat to cover the sudden sentiments.

"Yeah, that was a good day."

She's the only one who has ever been able to read my moods, and when she quickly changes the subject, I know that she hasn't lost her touch. "So, what the hell brings you here?"

I chew on my bottom lip, trying to remember. "A mystery tour?"

"Ah, shit. So those things actually do work. I paid a good chunk of change to get listed at the bottom of the night. It was totally worth it now," she says, smiling at me. "I've missed you!" She pulls me into another huge squeeze.

I pinch off the tears. There's no room for those here. "It's been a while," I admit. "How's it going?"

"Eh, it's going. A little tight for money, now that daddy's cut me off, but I'm getting by. How about you? I've heard the rumors. I don't believe any of them."

I'm not sure which rumor she's referring to, so I just brush it off. "Why not? They're all true."

She nods her head, smirking. "Okay then. I guess we really do have a lot of catching up to do then. Where are you staying?"

I try not to tell her I've just moved into a dirty, little hole in the ground, but I can't lie to her. "A scumbag motel on Victoria."

"You've got to be shitting me. I'm at the Dusty Rose across the street."

"What? You're staying in a motel?"

"The best money can buy," she teases. "I told you money is tight these days. It's a big place, though. Two adjoined rooms with a double bed in each. My roommate just bailed on me, and now I have to foot the whole bill this month. What about you? I thought you were living in a cozy little neighborhood in NYC."

I look to the floor to find the courage to tell her. "After Zayne died, I lost everything. I barely scraped by this past year. Zayne's insurance was audited. The company is probably looking for a loophole, so they don't have to pay me anything else. The bank has taken the house. I could barely afford the bus ticket to cross the country." I shrug my shoulders, and she keeps on listening. "The house was huge for one person, anyway. It was big enough for an entire family."

"Oh, Clarisse. I'm so sorry. You must have been devastated."

I just barely manage to stifle the tears pricking the back of my eyes. I nod my head but don't answer. I just barely manage to stave off the tears that have been haunting me for days now. The excess liquor certainly isn't helping.

"Losing Zayne was pure horror, but my baby boy? That's the hardest thing to deal with."

"Was it the accident that took him from you? I've heard other... *stories*."

I press my eyes shut and let the tears sting my eyes. "It was an accident—a terrible, terrible accident. Zayne Junior—" I shake my head with memories of that day flashing before my eyes. "It was the worst day of my life. When he died, what was left of my goodness died."

A tear trickles down Savari's cheek as she takes my hand and rests it on her heart. I feel a good cry coming on, but I feel like it's undeserved, so I suck back the emotion and keep a brave face. I accept the extended silence and take a few steadying breaths, before Savari breaks away from me.

"Hey, crazy idea. If you're not tied to the place you're staying at now, why don't you move in with me? You do plan to stay in the city for a while, right?"

The change of conversation is welcome, but I don't know if that plan is such a great idea. I came here to get away from my old life, but it seems to have found me again.

"To be honest," Savari adds. "I could use a little help with the rent. It'd be cheaper than what you're paying now, since I'm only asking you to pitch in what you can."

I think about it for only another second. I've only paid for one night, hoping something better would come along, although I did promise to pay for an entire week's stay.

"Come on. It'll be just like old times," she says, coaxing me to say yes.

"All right."

Her hands do a little cheer, but she doesn't make a sound, her maturity coming to the rescue. "Where are you working now, anyway?"

"Uh, hem," I say, clearing my throat sarcastically. "I just arrived in San Francisco today, and I'm unemployed at the moment. Finding a job is next on my list of things to do."

"Ah, right. Well, if you need a job, you're welcome here doing whatever you want. Can you bartend? We can always use help in the kitchen. Maybe you can help keep the books."

All of those options are lovely, except for one thing. "What I'd really like to do is dance."

"What?" Disbelief mars Savari's fair features.

"Is that so hard to believe? It felt good to be up there on stage tonight. With the spotlight on me, I thought about nothing but the music running through my body. I want to dance, if that's even an option."

"Shit." She smiles at me again. "You never cease to amaze me, woman. Training starts on Monday, but know that I don't hire just any random flabby chicks. Only the best of the best get on my stage. Tonight was nothing. Amateur night draws in a different crowd."

"I can do it. I've been exercising like a madwoman ever since—" Again I stop, reaching one of the many hot topics I prefer not to discuss.

Savari saves me the effort of trying to reword my situation. "I can see that. You look amazing. I'd never have known you were pregnant—" This time she's the one stopping. "I'm sorry, Clare. You've been through a lot. We need to talk, big time."

"It's okay. It's' no secret. I was pregnant. I lost the baby."

"That must have ruined you, delivering that baby all alone. I was so upset when I heard the news. It's not your fault, Clarisse, as long as you realize that. You do realize that, right?"

I shrug my shoulders, trying to change the topic. "The walk was my idea, but did you hear what my dumb-ass mother-in-law did?"

"No. What's that?"

"They buried my husband without waiting for my discharge."

Both of Savari's hands fly to her mouth. "Who would do such a thing?"

I shake my head. The proper question is not who, but why? Why is this kind of thing always happening to me? "Tell me again that I'm not cursed."

I see the pain in her eyes as she listens to my cold rendition of my living, breathing hell. "Savari, I swear I've never felt more wretched in all my life. First Zayne, then my baby boy." I stop talking. All this talk is too much. I've tried to bury this loss the deepest, and it seems to cut the sharpest when unveiled.

"I don't know how you've survived."

The special walls I've built in my head go flying back up. "Meds, lots and lots of sleeping pills, oh, and wine." I try to giggle but it comes out like a heart-breaking snort.

"Come here, girl."

When Savari opens her arms to me, I fall into them. I'm a sucker for love, feeling denied the real thing, by plenty fault of my own. "Oh, Clare," she whispers, hugging me tightly. "It'll get better for you. It has to. I'll do whatever I can to help."

I don't reciprocate her embrace long or hard enough, but Savari won't let go. "Give me a god-damned hug, woman. I feel so sorry for you."

"Well, don't." I lift my head from her shoulder as I push that horrible feeling deep inside my chest.

"I can't help it," she says. "It's not right. You've been put through the wringer a few times. How much can a girl take?"

"You're telling me."

Savari shakes her head. "Your luck changes today. You're going to move in with me, and we're going to live happily ever after. All right?"

My frown lifts into a playful smirk. "I take it you don't have a boyfriend."

"Nothing serious. This town is filled with cheating assholes, bisexuals, and men with ugly hearts."

I cringe, knowing I'm not one to help the situation.

"What's wrong?"

"I'm probably a disservice to intelligent women like you. I take a perfectly decent man, thrust my tits into his hands, and ruin his family."

"You'll fit in here just nicely," she teases.

"But I'm serious. I turn good men bad. I make average women pay for not respecting what they have."

"Hey, that sounds fair to me. If the woman isn't doing her job at home, that's her problem. If a man can't resist your tits, he doesn't deserve the good life."

I burst into laughter. "Savari, you make me smile so hard."

"Yeah, I am good for that."

"Are you saying my tits aren't amazing, though?"

"Those saggy momma tits?"

"You bitch," I say dramatically, making a sour face.

She belts out a laugh. "I'm only teasing. Your tits are beautiful. Any man able to resist you must be a magician or a homosexual."

Again, I laugh. "Oh, Savari, I really needed this."

"Cool. So, I'll ask Derek to swing by your place after his shift to pick up your stuff. What room did you say is yours?"

"Hold up. Derek, your security guard, Derek?"

"Yeah, he helps me with everything."

"Everything?" I ask, waggling my eyebrows at her.

She slaps me. "Not *everything*," she says, telling me

everything I need to know.

"You're lucky to have someone you can trust, but I don't need your hired muscle."

"Sure you do. Derek is exactly the help you need. He will carry your shit, and it doesn't hurt that's he's cute in the face."

"He seems like a nice guy."

"He is. He'll take good care of you... I mean, your things. He'll take good care of your things." She pauses and makes a pouty face at me. "You leave him alone."

My mouth drops open. "You did not just accuse me of trying to pick up your security guard."

"I like Derek. I don't want you to fuck him up."

"Oh, thank you very much, Miss Perfect."

"You know what I mean."

And I do. Everyone and everything I touch turns to shit or dies. "I promise to leave Derek alone."

"Thank you."

"I'll tell you what," I start, stretching my arms above my head in a dramatic fashion, because I hate to intrude on her night any longer. "I'm whipped. I'm just going to catch a cab home and crash. Give me a day to collect my bearings and we'll get together Monday night to decide what to do next."

Savari feigns disappointment. "All right. I'll see you Monday, lady."

"Not if I see you first, momma."

28: From Dusk Till Dawn

I 'm lying next to Devlin Decker, my back flattened atop a picnic table overlooking the bay bridge, the array of LED lights a permanent fixture illuminating the Bay Area sky. We're just far enough away that we're bathed in unsettling shadows, but neither of us is too worried about it.

"I'm glad you decided to join me tonight, Clarisse." His voice darkens. "Of all the men you could have left that club with…" He doesn't finish his sentence.

I know exactly what he's thinking, and I smile when I catch the way he watches me. Time to play devil's advocate. "About that." I stare up into the night sky. "If you could have your heart's desire—anything you ever wanted—right now, what would it be?" I turn toward him, my leg gently brushing up the length of his.

He stares into my eyes. "You. Without a doubt, you."

I shiver from the authority in his voice. He doesn't move or say anything more. I smile again and pull myself up so I can get him in between my legs. On my knees, I lower down until I'm sitting on his lap. He's still lying back, his eyes showing how intrigued he is by the progress he's making already.

My eyes settle on his. "Out of all the things you could have chosen—money, mansions, a lifetime supply of loose women—you picked me. Why?"

His eyes grow wide, like he can't believe I don't see the answer for myself. "You're beautiful, smart, flexible…" He pauses on that last word. "Friendly."

Mmm hmm. *Friendly.* I grab the hem of my shirt and lift it over my head, dropping it on top of his face so it blocks his view. I reach behind my back and unlatch my bra while Devlin fumbles to get free from my shirt. When he casts it aside, I'm already naked down to my waist.

"Do you like what you see, Dev?" If the size of his pupils are any indication, I'd say he likes it very much.

He nods his affirmation. I take his hands and cup them over my breasts, squeezing his fingers into my soft flesh. I arch my back until my hair dangles down and touches his thighs. With closed eyes, I imagine it's Parker's hands touching me, his hardness rising up to meet me. I drop my hands and moan when he keeps gripping my breasts. He moans, too.

I roll my head back and forth, keeping my eyes closed. "What if I said I want to give you everything you ask for?" I rub against him, the friction making him shiver.

"Yes," he breathes.

"Now," I say, prying open his pants, secretly confiscating the switchblade from his pocket before moving aside.

"Yes," he moans, pulling off his clothes frantically but leaving on his socks.

"Everything," I say.

Once he's good and naked, and the switchblade is safely tucked in the band of my thong, I take all his clothes, roll them up into a ball and toss them into the sand a good ten feet away.

"Now you," he says eagerly, lying back down. He reaches for my skirt, but I slap his hand away and wag a finger at him.

"Ah, ah, ah." I take my skirt off and toss it aside, but not until I've placed the blade on the picnic table between his legs.

He only notices how my thong is the only barrier between us. "Please," he begs.

"Do I look like the kind of girl who gives it up that easily?"

He snickers. "Sorry to say, Clarisse, but you kind of do."

Anger builds in my gut and flushes through my chest until it's stinging my eyes. I stare at him, willing my illusions to bring back Parker, but it doesn't work. It's only Devlin Decker and his substandard cock embracing the world around it. A breeze whispers through my hair, and I close my eyes, but when I open them, it's still Devlin—the selfish prick who called me a whore.

I look around for something to tie his wrists and turn up only one option. I stand on the seat of the picnic table, and pull off my thong. That'll do nicely. Devlin looks at nothing but me as I crawl over him. I pop his head through one of the holes to wrap the thong around his neck. I stretch the rest of the material out to bind his wrists snugly behind his head. A smart man would question my motives. He mumbles his appreciation.

"This is amazing." He laughs.

He won't be laughing for much longer.

I settle back on his thighs and wrap my hand around where he's hardest. I grip him gently while my other hand searches behind me for his switchblade. It's all there in his eyes—excitement mingling with desire.

"I think you have the wrong impression of me, *Dev*." I say his name with purpose, to disguise the sound of the blade switching open. My hand clutches him harder and he yelps.

"Hey. That hurts!"

I loosen up, so he doesn't freak out, but only for a second. "You mean this?" I crush him in my hand. If I hadn't have flashed the knife first, he wouldn't still be lying there in such a vulnerable position.

My evil laugh echoes down the beach and disappears into the darkness. He obviously values his balls, or he might've tried a little harder to get up. I point the blade at him in warning. That's right. Lie back down. You're not going anywhere.

"What are you doing? I don't understand." He stutters, "I-I-I thought we were having a good time."

I quirk an eyebrow and draw the blade closer to his face. "And then you called me names." I point the edge of the blade toward his neck, where I slowly draw a line below the band of fabric.

He blinks erratically, but he lies there very still as I mirror that line on the other side of his neck.

"Don't... Move," I whisper next to his ear. I can't help but smile when blood starts to leak from the seams. He has no idea what I'm doing to him.

He swallows and that only makes it worse. I draw my tongue over his neck and lap up the blood.

"You taste good."

He flinches when I reach between his legs.

"Relax." I stroke his flaccid penis. I wanted him hard for this. "This is going to be good." I lift up and his eyes flash to my naked chest, his mouth held partially agape.

I can tell he's still thinking about sex when I rub on him but he doesn't respond when I press my lips against his. "Kiss me," I order.

His mouth softens against mine, and I feel him stiffening once again in my hand.

I pause to smile. "That's more like it." Then I deepen our kiss, wishing it didn't have to come to this.

Devlin pulls away for a breath when I dig into his lip with my teeth. "You-you-you said you were going to make my dreams come true." Even after I cut him, he's still putting desire ahead of his life.

Big mistake.

If he wasn't so spoiled—so used to getting whatever he wanted—maybe he would have thought twice before inviting me out here and leaving his driver in the parking lot. Maybe after I pulled out the knife he should have tried to hurt me. That would have been fun.

This will be fun, too.

He struggles beneath me as I push the blade against the base of his manhood. "Sorry to break it to you, Dev. You can't always get what you want."

I stand from the picnic table when I hear a car door close in the nearby parking lot. I walk toward the sound, wearing nothing but a spray of Devlin's blood. The dark silhouette races toward me and stops a few feet away. I can hear his breathing from here, and I would recognize that tall frame and broad shoulders anywhere.

His voice shivers when he speaks. "Clarisse?"

29: It's Your Dime

I wake with a gasp, sitting upright in my bed, trying to make sense of the horrifying dream I had. I glance around the room feverishly, sweat pooling on my brow and soaking the clothes I'm still wearing from last night. It takes me a minute to register where I am. I moan when I realize the perma-gross scent has officially filled my nostrils.

My dingy motel room reeks.

I sigh, relieved that it was only a dream but frustrated to find something crusty seems to have permanently glued me to my sheets. I cringe at the thought and dive out of the bed, taking the sheets with me. I whip the crusty thing aside and have a mini panic attack on the floor from the grossness. On my hands and knees, I notice there's dried blood under my nails that I can't explain.

No. It was only a dream. It was only a dream.

I pinch my eyes shut and get to my feet. In the bathroom, I check my breath. Even after vigorously brushing my teeth for a minute straight, my mouth doesn't taste all that minty. It feels a lot like the mold growing on the sink. When I drag open the shower curtain, the base of the tub doesn't look a whole lot more appealing. I refuse to go in there barefoot.

Wearing nothing but my sandals, I climb into the tub and claw the bar of soap. Standing under a moderately warm spray of water, I quickly scrub the night off my body and end up losing the bar of soap to the moldy depths of the tub. My shower is quick, but I don't feel much cleaner than I did when I got in. I quickly exit the bathroom and pull on a pair of skinny jeans. While the jeans are tight, the shirt is light and airy. You might be able to see my black bra through the draped fabric, but I've yet to hear a man complain about it.

Rather than doing my hair, I flip my head upside down, finger comb it into a high pony and pile my hair atop my head with a few pins. I dig into my purse in search of my favorite cherry lip gloss, and coat my mouth with a shiny red color before I take off for the day.

I take a step outside and instantly pull on the sweater I bring along. The sun thought it'd trick me into thinking it was going to be warm outside today, but I'm not as naïve as I look. Zayne had told me stories about San Francisco, so I knew I could expect the grey skies and a cool wind. He thought I'd like it here because the sun doesn't shine that often, but the damn sunshine seems to have followed me here. At least the clouds follow me around and work quickly to cover it up.

Ignoring the strange weather, I focus on taking a deep breath. It feels good. The air isn't very fresh but my perspective is. I hastily call a cab, and wave it down as it drives right by me. The car tires screech as it comes to a stop not far up the street. I run toward the stopped car and let myself in.

"Where to?" the cabby asks me.

"The nearest convenience store, please."

He nods his head and yields into traffic without glancing at me. He veers into the left lane, making the person behind us lay on his horn. The gas pedal is dropped, and I'm forced backward against my seat until he lightens up the pressure to pull into a crumbling parking lot. It's not the best part of town, and the place isn't very well kept, but it's not like I'm a total gem myself at this time of morning.

He points at the corner of a dilapidated brick building. "It's right around there."

I probably could have walked here faster than waiting for the traffic to open up, but I act grateful for the ride. "Can you wait here, please? I'll only be a minute."

He points at his clock.

I give him a quick nod, jump out of the backseat and make a beeline for the front of the store, searching over my shoulder to check my surroundings. I shiver from the eerie feeling overcoming me. It feels like someone's watching me, and this isn't the first time I've felt this way since arriving in this city. Has someone followed me here?

My eyes rake across the street, but the only other people

I can see are a few loiterers in the small parking lot. Intuition has me maintaining a brisk pace. The pavement is stained with oil, and the brick wall is spray-painted with some funky design that looks pretty fresh. This isn't a place I'll hang out at for any length of time if I value my life. I pull open the door to the Piggy Mart and slip down a narrow aisle in search of a pack of gum. I settle on the minty fresh one and stop in my tracks when I see a man placing a few items on the counter.

I instantly recognize him from the night before. He's wearing the same ball cap and has the same dimples when he smiles. My eyes burn into him fiercely. I know that face intimately. He glances toward me. Before he can make eye contact, I quickly twirl away and walk down the next aisle, on the brink of a panic attack.

A million butterflies take flight in my chest. This isn't happening. My hands tremble with a mixture of fear and uncertainty. I move toward the front of the store slowly, hoping he'll be gone by the time I make it there. When I step around the display of sunglasses, I'm faced with another animal entirely.

Brooding. Enigmatic. Mr. Sexy. He's taken off his hat. Now he's all broad shoulders and dark, trimmed facial hair. I part my lips for a breath, moving toward the door, thinking of a way to get out of here without having to speak to him. He peels a five dollar bill out of his wallet and tosses it onto the counter before stepping backward to block my path to the door.

My heart stops when I realize he recognizes me. I drop the pack of gum to the floor and dive to the left just as he does the same. I make to go the other way, until we're dancing back and forth, our bodies growing closer with each of my attempts to escape him. We're face to face when I stop—close enough for me to know that his mouth smells like sizzling cinnamon.

I wait for him to say something—a, *What are you doing here?* Or maybe even, *What, you following me?*—but he doesn't. A playful smile makes its way onto his face. It's unexpected and devastating. No words, only the same smile I woke up to every morning for a good year. I fidget under his dark, assessing eyes.

I can't do this right now.

I push past him, but he grabs onto my wrist. "Let me go," I say, yanking my arm free.

He does as I ask, but I feel his sweeping glance all over my body. I hurry through the door to the parking lot where I find the taxi rolling backwards.

"Wait!" I scream.

It's a miracle the driver hears me, or maybe it's the frantic wave of my hands, but the car stops and I pour myself into the backseat and shout for him to, "Go! Go! Go!" I try to clear my brain to prepare for my audition at the Fox Shoppe, but his cologne hangs in my nostrils. It's an unmistakeable scent.

I give my head a shake and continue on as if nothing has happened, even though he is surely the only thing I'll be thinking about for the rest of the day.

"The Fox Shoppe. There!" I say to the driver while looking out the window. "Can you take me around back?"

The glowing neon sign from the other night is now dull and lifeless in the grey of the morning. The car pulls around the corner and rolls up to what looks like your typical dive bar. The brick on the building is clearly original and even though it's obvious that not a dime was spared on the flashy, neon signage out front, the back wall of the place is practically falling over. Brick crumbles from the wall and apparently someone thought painting the duct tape black would fix the eyesore of jagged metal framing the door. For the record, it doesn't help at all.

The back door is pretty fancy, though. It's solid black and there's a silver silhouette of a woman dancing on it, followed by the words, The Fox Shoppe. When I twist the handle to let myself in, it doesn't give. I pound on the door three times and cast a fleeting glance down the long alleyway. I check to make sure I'm alone, which I am as soon as the cab disappears into traffic on the next block over. I knock on the door again, and this time it squeaks open, but no one's standing there.

I think twice before stepping inside the dark room but decide to go for it. I enter the back door in search of the mysterious doorman.

Derek appears from the shadows with a smile on his face. "Did I scare you?" he teases.

I give him a look that makes him smile harder. "Not even close. Nice try, though."

"I'm only playing. The girls are in the other room." He points me in the right direction. "You're late."

"Fashionably," I answer, heading toward the only door with light on the other side of it.

He chuckles at me. "Right. I'm sure Savari will see it that way, too."

I flip my hair over my shoulder as I look back at him. "Sarcasm already. I can see we're going to be great friends."

Derek blushes, the balls of his cheeks turning forty shades of red. I turn away to give him some space while smiling about it.

"Through here?" I point toward another door, with my heels still clicking steadily.

"Yep," he answers, shaking the redness quickly. "Right through there."

We file into the room and stand at the back of the crowd. There has to be twenty girls in front of me, and every last one of them turns around to scope out the new competition. They all have their game faces on. I smile and casually twiddle my fingers at them to point out just how nosy I find them. One by one, they turn back toward the front of the room while Savari finishes her introduction.

I still can't believe there are actual tryouts, let alone cuts. I didn't know there was such an abundance of classy-looking women with low morals and a sharp wit. With a quick look around the room, I see that maybe this audition thing is no joke.

"Nice of you to join us." The baritone in Savari's voice stuns me and the girls spread apart like she has laser vision that will burn them if they don't clear out a path. She turns toward the ladies in the front row and they all watch her, like devoted disciples, as she walks toward me.

"Rule number one: you will arrive no less than fifteen minutes before our first choreographed dance of the night, whether you are scheduled to be on the stage or not. Capiche?" Savari flashes a glance of warning at me.

It wasn't necessary. I wouldn't test her authority in front of her staff, anyways. "Got it. I'm so sorry, Savari. It won't happen again."

"Rule number two: you will call me Miss Fox. There will be no exceptions to this rule. It is a show of respect and reminds everyone who is boss around here." She flashes me another look, as everyone else nods their head.

"Yes, Miss Fox. I apologize."

When she looks away, I take a breath and think to ask Derek whether that exception bullshit includes me too, but he elbows me in the side before I can say anything. Even with my pouty lips staring up at him, he manages to keep a straight face through it all. Savari lines up the first three girls, and a D.J. spins a track full of base. I have a hard time blocking a small smirk as the first girl takes the stage. I can see that Derek's finding it difficult, too.

Savari calls it a freestyle dance. We'll all get our turn. This girl mistakes *freestyle* for *free for all*. I'm not the only one snickering. This poor girl is really bad. She looks tacky, her moves trashy, borderline disgusting, and I'm just getting started. I mean, it's one thing to have your thong up your butt, but this girl's ass is eating her baggy white underwear for breakfast.

The next girl isn't much better. At first, I wonder if she even brushed her hair today. I quickly learn that she likely had. With all that hair flipping it's no wonder it's in knots. What can I say? Tryouts are a joke. I must be the only one here with any real talent, let alone flexibility and dance training. These other girls look like they've stepped straight out of high school, some timid, others skanky, many of them acting like they're having sex with the stage. It starts to look like I've dropped in on an audition for a poorly funded porno flick.

Two of the girls in front of me can't even keep a beat, and it's questionable whether they can even speak English. If you ask me, Savari has got her work cut out for her if she's going to make dancers of any of them. I'm ready to throw in the towel, when the redhead from the other night takes to the stage, but then a stormy bass booms over the speakers.

Shit. I spoke to soon. She doesn't even move until the words start, and I'm already mesmerized in anticipation.

The girl stands very still, her wine-stained lips matching the song about chains and love. I can't take my eyes off of her. She's gorgeous, for one, with long corkscrew curls of a vibrant red color that any woman would die for. At first, she looks down, and I'm just waiting for her to look at me. Then she flips her hair up and lifts her chest, arching her back. Our gazes collide as she moves her body, and she seduces me from across the room like I've been selected as her target. Her eyes speak to me as loudly as her body. When I glance at Derek, I find he's just as fascinated by her.

Candy rolls her head down, slowly, and curls fall in front of her face one at a time. Ask me why this is the most appealing thing I've ever seen and I couldn't tell you, but everything she does is laced with sex appeal. She hasn't even pulled off her shirt, and I'm ready to throw my last dollar bill at her to keep it going.

This girl is good!

Okay, so Candy is officially pegged as my only competition. Rather than waiting for my turn, I decide to show everyone that I can be just as alluring, even if my confidence is suddenly waning. I kick off my shoes, pull the pony holder from my hair, and leap onto the tall stage, shocking Candy motionless. With a body gifted to me by Mother Nature herself, I'm used to the boys gawking at my full mouth and child bearing hips, and what man doesn't like lean legs with a little junk in the trunk?

Red is shocked that I would be so bold to interrupt her and struggles to rebound now that I've captured everyone's attention. She fights for the spotlight, but all it took was that one second for her to lose her audience. Now, they're all mine.

My smirk flirts with the crowd as I rock my hips like they have a mind of their own. My body listens to the music but is guided by the waves of an erotic ocean. I stretch my leg up over my head and swing around the silver pole that the others must have thought was out of order. I work the crowd like only the best bitch can and jerk my head aside, right on cue with the music. I hook a leg around the pole and reach back into a bridge, showing everyone that dancing is only one of my many talents. Then I flip out of it, knowing how appealing it looks when my long hair flips around.

Facing the back of the stage, my hair runs like dark silk down my back, my body hitting the beats in sharp motions that demand everyone's attention. Within moments, I've made the decision to ease off my shirt and let it slip from my fingers, knowing it's all in the tease. Derek tries to look away, but he's mesmerized by me.

I spread my legs, slamming to the floor into the splits. It's not the easiest thing to do in jeans, but I'll lose a pair to the cause if it means showing up Candy. Derek's eyes look like they're about to pop from his head, as I take my bottom lip between my teeth and crawl toward him like I want it, wearing my skin-tight jeans and a black satin bra with crimson lace trimmings.

Savari claps her hands, and Derek seems to snap out of it as soon as the music cuts. "Yes, ladies! That is what I am talking about! Did you see what just happened here?" Savari asks the captive wannabes.

A young lady, who's questionably old enough to be dancing at a place like this, raises her hand. "Miss Fox," she says with a mousy voice.

"This isn't high school," Savari says pointedly. "Speak."

The girl points right at me with a short, baby pink fingernail. "That girl just stole the spotlight from the red-haired one."

Savari nods but waits for someone else to elaborate. "Yes and no. Anyone else?"

No one raises their hand. I know exactly what she's about to say, but I figure it's best that it come out of Savari's mouth.

"That redhead's name is Candy," she informs us. "And she was really rocking it. Everyone give her a hand."

Everyone in the room, myself included, erupts into applause.

"She was bang on with those moves, and right when you think it can't get any better, in walked Clarisse with those long, flexible legs to steal the limelight."

The girls are all nodding their heads, making me feel proud and empowered.

"You all have a little something different in you. Your task for tonight is to go home and figure out what that thing is. Here at the Fox Shoppe we deliver fantasies," Savari explains. "While one man will love Candy's hair, another won't. Where one man will be attracted to Clarisse's self-sufficient personality and dark sophistication, another will despise it. I've been in this business long enough to know that a successful dance club has more than one weapon. I need a whole belt of you if we want this business to stay at the top of the night scene."

Everyone is so spellbound by everything Savari does and says. I wonder when she became such a great public speaker.

"With every change of the song, I want my next girl to steal the audience and make every man and woman in the place forget about that last girl. I believe that we've found a few stars among you today." She glances at the stage and winks at Candy, but Savari—or should I say Miss Fox?—refuses to make eye contact with me.

I can see this is going to be fun.

"Tomorrow, I'd like to see what you think makes you unique to the stage," Savari says with pause for dramatic effect. "Thanks for coming out today, ladies."

The group erupts with applause, not knowing that the

hard part is just around the corner. Savari flips up a page on her clipboard where she had been jotting notes the entire time. A few agonizing minutes of silence pass before she starts hollering off names.

"Tonya, Tammy, Kristina, Nikki, Abbie, Lori, Jocelyn, and Cassandra, please form a line over here." Savari points toward the wall.

At first, I can't believe she hasn't called my name, but then I realize Candy too is standing with me and four other girls of differing heights and abilities.

"If I haven't called your name, please follow Derek. He'll show you to the fitness center where you will find a copy of your new meal plan, exercise regime, and scheduled choreography, assuming you make it through the remainder of your training with The Fox Shoppe."

"As for the rest of you," Savari starts, turning her eyes on the ladies whose names she called. "I would like to see each of you in my office. Please come in when I call your name."

Savari promptly disappears from the room while Derek helps me off the stage. I bend forward to slip my shoes on, hanging on to my shirt, as he leads the lucky ladies to the fitness center. Candy scowls at me, showing her jealousy in true colors, as she helps herself down from the stage and stomps past me.

"Tonya," Savari shouts, causing the adorable girl with an edgy haircut but a much too sweet smile to hurry toward Savari's office.

I'm the last of the chosen women to step out of the room, leaving the other girls fidgeting with their fingernails in waiting. It doesn't bode well for them. I'm almost sure they're getting the axe.

When I enter the fitness center, I'm surprised by how bright and clean it is. I pick up a nutritional calendar and give it a quick once over, wondering if I'm a lost cause after all. The plan requires that I eat three to four square meals a day. I haven't been doing a good job of that lately. Since I left New York, I've been living off of coffee, and when I do eat something, it's been chips and chocolate or ice cream sandwiches.

"Hey, Derek," I say, pulling him aside to whisper privately to him. "I don't know if I can do this."

"Sure you can. I believe in you." He pats me on the back like we're old pals and leaves me with a smile.

I exit the back door of the Fox Shoppe feeling nervous, and it has nothing to do with the darkening alleyway and my lack of companionship. I sure hope I can pull this off. I have a strong bark, but have I bitten off more than I can chew? I guess it doesn't much matter. This is my last chance. Without Savari, I'll be living in the streets within a matter of weeks. I have no other choice but to do this. My entire life depends on it.

30: And So We Meet Again

I wake in a cold sweat, and it's like it's happening again. Everything I've done comes rushing back to me. My hands feel wet with blood. It's my punishment for murdering them. I relive that night when that gun fired, the weight of Finlay's death bearing down on me. I remember Zayne lying on the ground in a pile of blood and bones. Then I remember Devlin bleeding out beneath me.

No!

I blink my eyes repeatedly, and Zayne and Devlin disappear, but the vision of Finlay sitting in bed next to me doesn't go away. He's sitting there with the barrel of a gun to his ear.

I'll do it. Don't think I won't.

Blinking away that final vision, I pull on a pair of old sweat pants and tie my hair into a tight knot. I flash a glance at the alarm clock and realize I fell back asleep after turning off my alarm. It's not like I *had* to get up, but I did want to get into a healthier routine, and that includes getting back into my early morning exercise plan. It sure beats the crap they have me doing at The Fox Shoppe.

I blow out a harsh breath as I pull on my running shoes. I need to get out of here and go for a run to clear my head and shed some of this tension in my neck. I try to focus on my last pleasant image of Zayne, the morning before he was taken from me, but I can't seem to drum up a happy image today. Being away from our house in New York has done exactly what I feared it would do.

My good memories are fading.

I pull on a hoodie, flip the hood over my head, and plug earbuds into my ears so I can listen to my favorite running music. I turn it up loud, thriving on the pain of my bleeding ear drums and the fact that I can focus on something else for a change. I warm up with a light jog, quickly picking up the pace. Oxygen rips from my lungs as I sprint down the sidewalk at full speed in hopes of stripping my head of all thoughts entirely.

When I squeeze my eyes closed, I see him—Zayne—at least what was left of him after the car ran him down. It makes me feel like I'm standing in the middle of an arena, and a team of hockey players are repetitively slapping pucks at my stomach. That's how much it hurts to remember Zayne in those last moments, right before I lost my baby. It's easier to forget—to tuck those memories away for private moments of remembering only—but the memory of Zayne will never leave me... until the unthinkable happens.

The image of Zayne transforms into broader shoulders, thicker legs, and winking dimples. If it stopped there, it would be okay, but then there's the unforgiveable attraction. Only Parker Varela could draw out such inexplicable sensations in me.

That man. This City. I knew I'd find him here eventually, but what are the odds that we would meet up in that racy club? How likely was it that we would walk into the same shitty little corner store at the same time? More importantly, what are the odds of us crossing paths again? The thought brings an undeserved smile to my face as screeching tires bring me back to reality.

I jump backwards with my hands raised to the sky, just barely moving out of the lane of speeding traffic in time to save my face. Fate has a cruel way of reminding me of my sins.

What is wrong with me? I stand here on the edge of the curb, my life swirling around me in a rush of ignorance and suggestion while another car trims every thread on my shirt. Parts of my body ache with the reminder of what it feels like to be hit by a car. What if I just did it? I could end it all right now. One step into the street and my life would be over. No more Black Widow.

No more Parker Varela.

I stare straight ahead, trying to get my gut to override my fear, when a new reflection appears behind me in a passing car window. I spin around to see whether this is all in my head, but he's still there, in the distance. It takes a minute for my breaths to catch up to the irregular pattering of my heart. Parker snares me with a glance, numbing the pain and helping me forget.

He's standing very still with his hands buried in his jean pockets. I wonder whether he's truly there or just a figment of my imagination. I want to call out to him but don't know what I'll do if he answers back. Sweat teases over my forehead. The brisk wind hardens my nipples. I turn back toward the busy street, leaving my previous decision alone and focusing on a new one.

Run like hell.

I wait for an opening and sprint across the road, running as far away as I can, pushing my body to its limits, until my legs scream, and I have nothing left in me. As soon as I stop, I peel over in a fit of mental and physical exhaustion. I squeeze my eyes closed and pinch off tears that are trying to publicize my issues. Now is not the time for that.

I dig deep for air and walk it off, taking a different route back to my motel. I assess my surroundings when I notice a man turning the block behind me. If I didn't know any better, I would say Parker is still following me. This is not happening. This is not happening.

This is not happening.

I try to ignore him as he gains on me, but when I glance back at him, he snares my eyes with that familiar smile again. The way those dimples strike me and the way his eyes sweep over my rear end remind me how long it's been since I've let a man like him pleasure me. My body burns for touch. No. This is not real. I'm making this up. I refocus on breathing and stare at the ground. When I look up, he's gone from the sidewalk.

I knew it!

"Am I catching you at a bad time?"

"Shit!" I jolt upright while he smirks about catching me off guard. "Do you always sneak up on people like that? You could've given me a heart attack." I force a scowl when he moves closer to me Does he really need to smell my armpits? I gasp for air, now starved of it, seeing how close he is to me. A phantom side stich has me bending forward again; at least that's what I tell myself. It's all I can do to avoid his mesmerizing eyelashes.

"The only person having a heart attack here is me." Parker doesn't disguise his thorough assessment of my ass. "You really shouldn't be sticking that booty out there," he informs me, making me stiffen my spine and spring upright.

"Want a piece of advice?" he asks, without waiting for my answer. "You're not bulletproof. You *will* get yourself into trouble in this neighborhood with that thing." He nods in the direction of my rear-end like it's an amusement park ride. The erotic tone in his voice makes my body tingle in places that haven't had enough attention lately.

I clear my throat and say, "This is nothing. Seriously, I'm wearing stinky sweats and a pair of old runners. I'm at no risk in this neighborhood at this hour." The only person I fear will make trouble for me here is *him*.

With a quick glance, I reassess my surroundings. When I look back, I find the darkness in his eyes hasn't subsided. I need to find a way to get that dangerous look out of eyes. I don't like the places it makes me tingle.

I swallow hoping to moisten my dry throat. "I don't remember you being a morning person." I'd say anything to get him to quit looking at me like that.

"I could say the same thing to you right now," he answers, looking to my mussed up hair.

Little does he know, I've been out every day this week at this hour, trying to stick to Savari's rigorous training schedule. In fact, my next stop could almost be pegged to the minute. I race up and down the same sidewalk every day and then speed walk to the park around the corner. I would usually saunter around the grounds three times, leaving me enough time to cool down before I hit the small coffee shop for my morning dose of caffeine. I can't believe how predictable I've become.

Has he been watching me all this time?

That thought forces me to meet his eyes again. Damn, but those are naughty Varela eyes. What is he doing here? I know he feels the electricity between us. He shouldn't be here. *I* shouldn't be here.

I open my mouth and snap it shut before saying, "I really should go."

He lifts his eyebrows, like he's an innocent man. "I thought maybe we could grab a coffee, first. You quit returning my calls. I worry about you."

"Yeah. Not ready to go there right now."

He reaches out for my hand and holds it. He strokes my knuckles with his thumb, once. "I know why you sent me off. I get it."

I feel frozen in place, but shake my head with downturned eyes to break free from the grip his passion has over me. Does he know, really? My late husband would be rolling in his grave if he knew the feelings I started to have for his brother. I read on the internet that this is a normal response after the death of a loved one. I was trying to fill a void. That explains how I felt then. What about now?

Parker warming my bed would be my greatest mistake. I'm still wearing my husband's ring on a chain around my neck when I picture all that man lying naked in my sheets with pink cheeks and a glistening chest.

Parker's grip tightens on my hand, making muscles across my body squeeze and release. His lips move closer toward mine, his breath rushing over my skin. I should stop him, but I don't look up, my eyes remaining half-mast, my entire body curious to see where this crazy ride will take us.

His lips brush gently against mine. It's an innocent kiss—over before it even started—but it takes my breath away. I soon realize that's all he has in store for me. My eyelashes flutter upwards until our eyes meet. He's got me in a daze.

A dimple appears on his handsome face. "Hey, you still there?"

I gasp for a breath, my eyes flashing away to stare at the place on my hand where the small gold band used to sit on my ring finger. I jam my fist into the pocket of my hoodie and tear my other hand away from him, my shock wearing off in an instant.

"Look, I can't do this right now." I briefly look for traffic and jog across the road as soon as it clears, shouting back to him. "I'm sorry!"

I decide to cut across another road and get back on schedule. I can't let this ruin me. I can't let *him* ruin me. That's exactly what would've happened if I had stuck around to see where it would take us. Since I've shown up in San Francisco, things have changed for the better. I have a friend, the prospect of a good-paying job, and a respectful body guard. I'm still staying at a shitty motel, but that changes today. I will not let this set me back.

I jog to the park and make two passes around the pathway, deciding to skip the third pass. That dose of caffeine can't come soon enough today. I enter the café, take my usual seat near the window, and order a coffee. "A large, please."

I'm still struggling to answer why I feel the way I do while I unlatch the necklace holding my wedding band and dangle it before my eyes to inspect the cheap gold ring. With a sigh, I clutch the small circle in my hand and slide it into my sweater pocket. I know it's time I face the fact that Zayne is never coming back, but why now? Why today?

I flatten my hand atop the table and stare at my splayed fingers, glaring at the naked band of skin where my ring used to sit. My finger looks empty without it.

"Sorry to interrupt," the waitress cuts in.

I shove my empty hand into my pocket as the waitress lowers my coffee to the table, the hot liquid sloshing over the side of the stained mug.

"Thanks," I mumble sarcastically as the girl walks off.

I dry up the mess with napkins from the dispenser and glare at my coffee, as if that will cool it faster. I need that good stuff in my mouth. I lean forward and inhale the delicious fragrance, as it rises up to my nostrils. This diner is the one place I can relax. I've appreciated this seat every day this week, because it's tucked off to the side, overlooking the park. Everyone always leaves me alone, here. I wouldn't be so lucky today.

I'm blowing on my drink when my eyes flash forward. What the fuck? Parker is coming through the door. He avoids my gaze but I don't stop watching him. He saunters right toward me.

Parker doesn't sit at my table, but he might as well have. He takes the seat at a small table next to me, which is just as close if not closer. I turn away, my heartbeat taking off in a gallop.

What is he doing here?

I stare into the window and ignore the reflection, but even with my back to him, I can feel his eyes on me.

Is he trying to intimidate me?

I swivel around and scowl at him. He whistles a non-probing tune, with his hands clasped on the table in front of him. *He's ignoring me.* As if he's waiting for someone else to join him.

Yeah, okay.

I continue to stare at him, knowing the act all too well, until I connect with a startled chestnut gaze.

"Oh! Fancy meeting you here," he says.

"You followed me." Could he be any more obvious?

"I did no such thing."

I don't for one second believe the incredulity in his facial expression or his choice of words. "Really?"

"I may have seen you taking your seat, but this happens to be my favorite place."

I roll my eyes and brush a hand across my sweaty brow. "I can't believe this."

"If I'm bothering you, I can move." He makes to stand up, and I instantly feel the emptiness rushing toward me.

I lift a hand to stop him. "No. This is a public place. I can go."

He nods toward my full cup. "Don't leave on my account." He then pulls out his cell phone and resumes ignoring me.

I huff. *Fine.* I don't mind watching him through the

reflective glass, anyway. He is easy to look at, but it brings memories back to me that I thought I'd lost forever. I take the first taste of my coffee and try to sink into relaxation. "Mmm," I sigh.

I hear his chair scrape across the floor, and soon Parker's sitting in the chair across from me.

"Uh, can I help you?" I ask crisply.

"You really think you're going to get away with that?"

"With what?"

"Mmm," he moans, pulling out his best feminine mockery.

I burst into laughter. "That is not me."

"You're a man-eater," he says, as if this should be news to me.

I tease him before I can even stop myself. "Don't you wish that were true in the literal sense?"

One of his eyebrows pops up in erotic suggestion. That look is enough to make any heterosexual woman want to kiss his face off. I guzzle my drink and push the mostly empty cup into the middle of the table.

"Have dinner with me," he orders.

"Look, our little visit today has been fun, but—"

Before I can finish my sentence, he leans in and presses his lips against mine again. I try to fight it, but it's really tempting to lose myself in him. He doesn't let up. We're in public for God's sake. He sinks in that kiss and holds on to my face until I relent Not only do I surrender to his mouth moving against mine, but I kiss him back. He tastes of chocolate and cinnamon. Desire snakes through my body and hints for me to warm things up a notch, but I know better!

I pull free from his grip and catch the intimate expression on his face before he opens his eyes. That one small gesture leaves me even more confused.

"I've got to go." I glare at the few dirty singles I pull from my pocket and slap them onto the table. I hastily leave him sitting there before his eyes even get the chance to search mine for an answer.

"Wait!" he calls after me, but I don't stick around to see whether he'll follow me again.

I quickly replace the sound of his plea in my ears with music, and then I jog all the way back to my motel room with a worried smile on my face.

Some things in life are better left unsaid.

To be continued...

Learn more about Wicked Intentions online at http://christasimpson.com/wicked-intentions, or keep reading for a sneak peek at Chapter One!

1: Bad Habits

I scan over my dark motel room, but it's a waste of my time. I know I have everything safely inside my bag where it has remained all week so it doesn't catch cooties. I don't dare check under the bed again. Even if I had unpacked, it wouldn't take me long to pack back up. I don't own much, and what I do own is mostly clothes and hair products. This is nothing new. I've always believed, *the less you have the better*. For every time I decide it's safe to call something mine, it disappears or dies.

It's just like when I decided I could take my college life back into my own hands. Finlay died. I thought it was safe to call Zayne my husband—the father of my child—but I couldn't save him. I couldn't save either of them. They were doomed from the start—just like me. I can't protect myself from the cruel fate I seem to have been dealt, no matter how hard I try.

It's the curse of the Black Widow.

I don't like to buy into all that hocus pocus, but it's the only logical explanation. Why else am I alone, again?

"Yoo-hoo, Clarisse?"

"Oh!" I catch Derek's large shadow stretching into my room through my open door. "Hey, Derek."

"Is this it?" he asks, picking up my single black bag and walking it out to his trunk.

"That's it," I tell him while I lock the door behind me. I head for his car and stretch my arms toward the sky.

Derek slams his trunk and stares at me again. At first he's just noticing the way my shirt separates from my skirt when I raise my arms, and then he shakes that off and pays real attention to me. 'Everything okay?"

I hate how intuitive he is. "Yeah, I'm good," I lie.

He opens up his car door and looks back at me. "Then what are we waiting for?"

I glance toward the registration office. Even with the

light on inside the small room, there's a layer of dust filtering the view. "You go on ahead. I'll be right back."

"Are you sure? It's getting pretty late. I can wait."

"I'm sure. Don't worry about me. I'm not afraid of the dark, but I am low on cash. I'm going to run down to the Piggy Mart to visit the ATM real quick."

"Hop in. I'll drive you."

I shake my head. "Thanks, but I could use the fresh air. I'll be back before you know it."

He nods at me. "You want to be alone. Got it." He salutes me and gets into his car. "Be careful," he says, before closing his door.

I watch the navy blue car cross the four-lane highway, with the moon glimmering off the sparkly paint job. The red of his brake lights fills the night. Before Derek changes his mind and hollers at me to skip the ATM, I readjust the purse hanging from my shoulder and hurry down the sidewalk toward the Piggy Mart. The ATM is on the other side of the building, and I find it lit up like the fourth, with colorful spotlights and a dull street lamp hovering above it. Otherwise, the parking lot is dark—like, really, super dark.

I glance around but appear to be alone when the single car parked at the store takes off. I shrug my shoulders and then smirk at myself for worrying at all. Derek's just overprotective. I step into the spotlight, pull open my bag, and scoop out my wallet. As I plug my debit card into the machine, I notice an exchange of lights in the reflection of the panel. I freeze in place and remain very still, until I see the shadows moving oh so slightly.

If I didn't know any better, I'd say there is someone behind me, and I'm guessing from the bulky stature that the large shadow belongs to a man. I squint into the monitor to get more details, but the screen starts to time out. I quickly punch in my number, hoping that I'm dreaming this up, but no. I sense him moving closer, and I suddenly wish I was wearing more clothes.

When I cautiously check over my shoulder, I see it's definitely a man. He's wearing a hooded, long-sleeved shirt.

I try to see his face, but he stands just clear of the lamplight, making for damn sure anything his hood exposes is hidden by the shadows. Pepper spray would come in handy right about now. It's too bad I left that in my other bag.

I wait for the machine to process my withdrawal request, hoping this guy will leave, but an eerie feeling nags at me to forget about the money. I should run back to the safety of Derek's company. I ignore my instincts, knowing I have a wild imagination and an even worse track record with judging people. Maybe he's just waiting for me to finish with the machine.

Something tells me it's more than that.

It doesn't matter. I'm not leaving. I will wait for my money out and then get the hell out of here. With a deep breath, I relax a little.

The man doesn't make a move or a sound. Instead of sticking to the plan, I find myself twisting around to check him out. He quickly twists away. Is he intentionally hiding his face from me? A chill passes over my arms. I rub them quickly to shake the sensation washing over me as I face forward to check my balance.

"Shit!" My latest deposit hasn't cleared yet, and I don't think the $93.92 left in my account is going to cover the balance of this week's rent.

As I contemplate what I'm going to do next, staring at the pavement next to me, I notice the man's shadow blending into mine. The tall, dark figure moves up behind me, a little too close for comfort. My heart beats erratically as I ask the machine for my last four twenties. I hesitantly peer over my shoulder while the machine lines up the bills. I worry that I'm going to be attacked, my eyes finally connecting with the man's shadowed face.

I swallow and turn back to the machine. This is even worse than I had imagined. The man presses against me, just as my money starts spitting out. I barely stifle my gasp as he brings his mouth close to my ear.

"Don't move."

I roll my eyes. "Or what?"

"Do as I say and no one will get hurt," he says intimately.

I sigh out of amusement. "I've heard that before, on every crime show right before the criminal blows the victim's head off. Go nuts. I dare you to try and see what happens."

He slides something long and hard against the small of my back. "If you don't shut your mouth, I might be forced to do something I don't want to."

I use sarcasm as a crutch, recognizing the feel of the cold barrel against my skin. "Is that a banana in your pants, or are you just happy to see me?"

He doesn't lighten the pressure. "Take the money."

I glance at the little tray with the four bills hanging out. I don't even hear the incessant beeping noise until he tells me to pay attention. I quickly pull the twenties free and slide them into my wallet.

He wraps around me and growls in my ear, with his hands clutching me confidently, his warm cinnamon breath washing over my skin. "You'll follow me if you know what's good for you."

My left eyebrow quirks up at such a dark suggestion, and I absorb the thrill of him acting so menacingly. The man knows me too well. If he had approached me as a gentleman with a friendly question, the answer would have been no, but when he licks that full lower lip with that hooded glance, it gives me a chill and not an unpleasant one.

I can't decide whether he's trying to take advantage of me with fear or seduce me for romance, but when his breath on my ear makes me shiver, I feel it tingle across my entire body. I need to stop thinking these thoughts, but my breathlessness only brings that wickedly sexy smile back to his mouth. Without asking, he takes my elbow and pulls me toward the back alley. I don't fight it.

What am I doing, exactly?

I know any reasonable person would be screaming for help and kicking him in the balls. Unfortunately, I can't mess with such big, handsome balls. Eh, worst case scenario, he takes me from this cruel world. Best case, we have some amazingly hot sex.

He forces me around the back corner of the nearest building and presses me into the warm bricks as his mouth crashes into mine. He quickly slips his tongue past my lips and tastes me, his hands scouring my thighs and gripping on to them with large, masculine hands. When he thrusts forward, I feel the way he fills those jeans. He gasps for a breath and hooks on to my eyes, but he doesn't even need those long, dark lashes to lasso me in. I'm already roped.

That look has him devouring my mouth, my neck, and his hands seem to have a mind of their own. He grips me again, his hands then sliding up my thighs and in between them. He touches me like he'll never get to touch me again. If that's what he's thinking, he's probably right. Guilt gnaws at the corner of my mind. I start looking away, but he snares my gaze with those delicious chestnut eyes. A gentle movement of air cools my face, but it doesn't help the slow burn that is officially consuming my body.

Is he letting me go? That would be best. Well, not the best for my exploding ovaries but best for my conscience. He smirks at me. Still, we don't exchange a single word.

He's not letting me go anywhere.

Pick up your copy of Wicked Intentions today and get the crazy finale readers are *dying* to get their hands on!

"Day by day, piece by piece, he puts it all together. What will happen when he finally realizes what I've done?"

-Clarisse Blackwell

Support This Author
LEAVE A REVIEW!
(Please, no spoilers.)

GOODREADS
www.goodreads.com/christasimpson

OTHER CHANNELS
www.christasimpson.com/playing-house

Join Christa's Author Newsletter to receive special news, sneak previews, limited-time freebies, and exclusive offers right in your inbox.

See what you're missing out on!
http://christasimpson.com/newsletter

About the Author

Christa Simpson is a Bestselling Author who entertains her readers with protective alphas, sassy heroines, and a fast-paced storyline. She writes wicked steamy contemporary romances and erotic thrillers loaded with passion, suspense and sarcasm. In her free time, she loves reading, writing, music, movies and dancing.

Christa is a small town Canadian girl living in Tilbury, Ontario, with her husband and two beautiful daughters. She's a dreamer and has always believed you can do anything you set your mind to.

Please visit her website for more info:
http://christasimpson.com/about

Author of . . .
THE TWISTED TRILOGY
TWISTED DESIRE
THE DESTINY SERIES
TOUGH LUCK: A Forbidden Romance
DARK SECRETS, A Duet

A Note from the Author

Hey, you. Thanks so much for reading my book! I hope you aren't too upset about the cliffy, because this story needed to be told but was too wild, crazy, and thrilling to squeeze into one novel. I assure you that Wicked Intentions, book two in this dark, erotic duet, will answer all your lingering questions. If not, you can contact me directly to demand an explanation! I don't bite.

Honestly, I'm always looking for people just like you to join my VIP Reader's Group. If you enjoy my books, or are a voracious reader, you should seriously consider becoming an active member of my PRIORITY READERS team today. Try it out for free! You can start enjoying the perks immediately, and I promise not to spam you. Good stuff only! **http://christasimpson.com/review-team**

What more can I say? You must read Wicked Intentions to understand the true reason behind me publishing this story. I'll tell you now, some of the horrifying shit in this book you're thinking *has to be* completely fictional, I've experienced firsthand. There, I said it. It feels good to finally get that off my chest, but don't ask me which parts because I won't tell you. Then again, maybe my loose lips will share more at the end of book two. Hope to see you there!

~ Christa

Other Books by Christa Simpson

Acknowledgements

Okay, I'd like to drop a quick thanks or three before I go...

To my right-hand woman, my bestie, my beta, my girl. Sometimes I wonder how many times I can thank a single person, but you really are my SFAM. I always trust your opinion, rely on you to give it to me real, and love that I have a virtual shoulder to lean on whenever I need one. We will meet in person someday soon. I promise!

To Lori, my very first beta reader *ever*, who I know doesn't even read my kind of stories on a regular basis. Your input on this one was beyond amazing. If it wasn't for you and your support, I might not have had the courage to start publishing all those years ago. My thanks will never be enough. Much love!

To Lia, my editor. What a relief to know she has my back. If it wasn't for her, you would be stuck reading a rather large quantity of Canadianisms. Odds are many of you wouldn't have a clue half the time what I was talking about. Lol. Cheers to that!

Last but not least... you—yeah, you! Thank you so much for taking the time to read my story. You didn't have to do that but you did. I appreciate it.

Don't be a stranger. I'm happy to connect with you on social media, and I hope to see more of you there!

~ Christa Simpson <3

The Dark Secrets cast returns in...

WICKED INTENTIONS

www.twitter.com/blackwidowpub
www.facebook.com/blackwidowpublishing

www.ingramcontent.com/pod-product-compliance
Lightning Source LLC
Chambersburg PA
CBHW050839180626
46814CB00007B/2544